HOUSE OF THE NINE DEVILS

Johannes Urzidil

HOUSE OF THE NINE DEVILS

Selected Bohemian Tales

Translated from the German
by David Burnett

TWISTED SPOON PRESS

Prague

2022

ISBN 978-80-86264-60-8
ISBN 978-80-86264-62-2 (e-book)

This translation was supported by a grant from
the Federal Ministry of Arts, Culture, Civil Service and
Sport of the Republic of Austria and a grant from the
German Translators' Fund as part of the program
NEUSTART KULTUR by the Federal Government
Commissioner for Culture and Media.

Federal Ministry
Republic of Austria
Arts, Culture,
Civil Service and Sport

CONTENTS

House of the Nine Devils · 7

Vacation in Flames · 20

New Year's Commotion · 42

Porter Kubat · 63

We Stood Honor Guard · 84

The Last Tombola · 89

The Assassin · 118

A Night of Terror · 123

One Last Deed · 141

Step and Half · 164

Paternal Prague · 180

*Translator's Afterword: "Poverty
Is Splendor from Within"* · 192

HOUSE OF THE NINE DEVILS

When I was a child, there lived in the House of the Nine Devils, at the foot of Prague's Lesser Town, nearby the Moldau island of Kampa, an old woman of nearly a hundred years whom my father visited from time to time. He would take me along when he did, since my father was a widower and rarely had anyone to leave me with. As a student in the seventies he had lived in that very house. It was situated near a canal called "Čertovka," or Devil's Stream, that divides Kampa from the mainland. The old woman, already advanced in years during my father's student days, had been his landlady at the time. He had come from the German-speaking part of western Bohemia to a strange, seemingly gigantic and somewhat uncanny Prague, and this woman, to whom he'd been recommended, had looked after him like a mother, which explained his lasting attachment to her.

There was another reason for these visits, though: the old house itself, with its narrow, angular stairs, its many adjoining chambers, alcoves, cabinets, secret doors, and maze-like rooms in the cellar, and whose mere name seemed demonic. No one lived in the building except the old spinster, who'd been appointed by the owners — Bohemian nobles of old aristocratic stock — as the caretaker, a position her father had held before her, even though there was nothing to take care of in this house apart from the rooms the caretaker occupied. The other rooms were empty, or at least unoccupied. Here and there were perhaps the odd piece of rickety furniture, some strange contraption or other whose sole remaining purpose consisted in growing old, a worn and ratty armchair that was only fit for weightless ghosts, a warped bookshelf with a few shriveled pigskin volumes on it. In sooty kitchens, layer upon layer of verdigris and patina formed on bronze and copper, pewter decomposed from leprosy and disintegrated from the plague, three-legged iron cauldrons acquired a scab of brittle rust.

On each of his visits my father would roam these musty rooms, wandering from floor to floor all the way to the attic, which was full of endless quantities of junk, crates without lids, gaping trunks, absurdly shaped bottles and giant balloon flasks, between which a tilted Earth globe, a celestial globe, and a bronze coelo-tellurion had always piqued my curiosity. But more than anything my father liked to go down into the vaulted two-story subterranean cellar, a burning candle in one hand, me hanging onto the other, a cellar that was home to metallic residues, crucibles, mortars and pestles, iron bowls and copper scales whose joints the oxides of time had naturally encrusted and whose rafters and other structures had been bandaged together by thick cobwebs. There was nothing particular my father was looking for, and he hardly ever touched a thing; he was merely there to observe, as if all these abandoned and forgotten objects occasionally needed a human glance in order to continue existing. Hardly a word was spoken during these explorations.

But when you entered the little old lady's small ground-floor apartment an entirely different world opened up, a well-tended cosmos organized down to the smallest detail, in which each of the old Elbogen or Schlaggenwald porcelain cups, each piece of Haida cameo glass, each lace doily was subject to its own order and rules. It was not so much a living space as a precise apparatus for attaining the greatest possible security and dependability in day-to-day life. Everything was always in its place, and my father explained to me the virtues and merits of such a clearly structured way of living, where you never had to look for something and were never at a loss when you couldn't find it. And in the midst of this almost solemn structure made up of hundreds of necessities, or superfluities raised to the status of necessities, looked after by the most incomprehensible ornamental objects that, in turn, were looked after by her — in the midst of this sat the little old lady in almost preternatural spotlessness, well arranged in her rocking chair, a piece of lacework perched atop her sparse white hair, a broken ruff above the black silk mantilla, clad in an immaculate white apron, her feet in buckled shoes propped against a carved footstool.

No sooner had I bowed and whispered my timid greeting than she raised her gray, knowing hand — a hand versed in ancient things, covered with countless furrows, with wrinkles and brownish spots — and gently caressed my forehead with it. It did me good, for in my boyhood there was no one else who would have ever done this. My father never felt so inclined, was probably too introverted. He was sad, my father, and rarely came out of his sadness, except when he told a story and found himself getting carried away, which was probably quite literally the reason he told stories.

The old woman sometimes told stories too. And then the primeval hills and valleys of her countenance came to life or even blossomed, her eyes, like two lamps, seeming to illuminate the objects around her, revealing their otherwise shadowy qualities, and her lips, pleated by time, gained color.

Next to her on the little table stood a golden oval frame with a hand-sized half-length color portrait of a handsome gentleman in a high-necked coat with a star-shaped medal. Once, after a visit, my father told me he'd kill to have that portrait but would never dare even broach the subject, because he knew that not for anything in the

world would she ever part with it, linked as it was to the most important event of her life.

"Who's it a picture of?"

"She never mentioned his name, probably doesn't even know it.
But I have an inkling."

"What kind of inkling?"

"You should never talk about mere inklings," said my father, "that's
the business of poets."

"And what about the event? Do you know anything about it?"

"I do. I had something to do with it. But that was a long time ago.
I'd have to think about it and try to piece it together. But before I do,
you should know something about the house itself. I spent four years
of my life there. The house means a lot to this city."

"Of course, if you lived there."

"Back then it was just as empty or, rather, full of junk as it is today,
only there were two other furnished rooms: one for the old woman's
crippled father, and one for renting out. That's where I lived, and even
in those days I used to sneak from floor to floor, rummage through
the attic and explore the cellars."

"Did you find anything?"

"Well, nowadays I would probably find lots of things that seem
valuable to me. But not back then. That's what time does. It creates
value. At least as much as it destroys. Remember that."

I remembered it, the way we best remember those things that we
understood the least.

"But I did find something there once," Father continued. "That
little portrait that means so much to the old woman. How that happened, and where I found it, that's the story that ties me to this house.
I'll get back to that in a moment. The old woman shrieked when I
brought her the portrait. She threw her arms around me, kissed me,
rejoiced, started to sing and even to dance, despite the fact that even

in those days she could have been my grandmother. That was on a weekday, but still she roasted me a knuckle of veal and rolled the best apple strudel of my life."

"The portrait must have really meant a lot to her."

"For sure. But to know why, you have to know a lot of other things. In the old days, four hundred years ago, a famous black magician was said to have lived in the House of the Nine Devils. There's another house in Prague, on the south side of Charles Square, that's linked to the name of Faust. The legends say this and that. Maybe he lived in both of them, maybe in neither. At any rate, they say he was born in Bohemia, probably even in Prague. Others, who don't care much for Bohemia and Prague and always pretend they know everything better, would like to think he was born in Swabia. None of that matters much nowadays. But this Prague, where you too were born, is an old city of magic. This is where the rabbis had their sorcerer's apprentices and where the emperors kept their alchemists. Many things came together here — East and West, Jew and Christian, Czech and German, North and South — and where many essences converge, many wondrous, inconceivable things come to pass: things, words, characters and occurrences that have never been seen before. It's a breeding ground for spells and magic powers."

"And what kind of magic tricks did this black magician do? Did doves fly out of his sleeves? Did he saw a woman in half in midair?"

"None of those kinds of gimmicks. He was a scholar, a learned doctor. He produced rejuvenating medicines or ones that allow you to age indefinitely, he concocted gold from base metals, but most of all he conducted experiments to create an artificial homunculus. Many attempts have since been made in Prague. Fifty years after the doctor, the famous Rabbi Loew set in motion his mechanical servant, the Golem. But the doctor had had something else in mind. Using all kinds of elixirs and gases, he tried to create a living being inside a big balloon flask, and supposedly succeeded in part, in league as he was with one of the nine devils. But one devil alone is not enough. You have to have the whole confederation on your side: Mephistopheles, Cozintras, Asmodi, Trochadeus, Astharot, Serpens, Beelzebub, Samael, and Fofunagra, or as they say in Czech: Fanfrnik. I know their names by heart. They're part of the house. Of course, over the centuries, the house has been rebuilt a number of times and now looks completely different from the outside than it did when the doctor lived there. It belonged to the same noble family as it does today, and the owner in those days, a royal chamberlain, had placed it at the doctor's disposal to use for his own purposes. Other sorcerers and gold-makers moved in after him. But inside, the rooms have remained the same, complete with the tools and equipment from the century of magic. Some of these may have even belonged to the doctor himself, and it's entirely possible that one of the green balloon flasks lying around in the attic may have housed his homunculus."

"Why do you actually need artificial humans?" I asked. "Aren't there enough natural ones?"

"Science doesn't ask what the results are good for," explained my father sternly. "One of its principal tasks is to create artificially what nature with little effort produces on its own. All of this leads to God, whom man tries to compete with. It would take me hours to explain. Back in the days when everyone believed in God, people thought there must be a devil involved in such undertakings. Those were still the good old days. Nowadays engineers don't believe in God or the devil."

My father was an engineer himself, and invented and designed all sorts of things. To me he seemed to be somewhere in the middle, between the old-school devil's disciples and the new brand of technicians, still believing in the possibility of a God but ruling out the existence of devils. He still belonged to the spirit of the previous century. "And the portrait," I asked him, "tell me about the portrait."

"Maybe," he said after thinking it over, "it's best I tell you the story in her words, the way the old spinster told it to me one quiet evening after the death of her father. Back then there were nothing but quiet evenings. That was over twenty years ago, but her room looked the same as it does now, and she herself was already pretty old. Her face, her neck, and her hands were almost as wrinkled as they are today. So what was the story she told me?"

"I was still a child, barely thirteen, it was the year the Frenchman was defeated at Leipzig. Anyone out of the cradle by then remembers that year exactly. Even before the battle, the city was full of strangers, especially wounded soldiers from the coalition armies — Austrians, Prussians, Russians. They were lying around all over the place, not just in people's apartments, but in the entranceways and stairwells too. We were the only ones not quartering anyone. People shunned the House of the Nine Devils, no one would put their wounded here. They feared the wounds wouldn't close, that the pain wouldn't go away in this accursed house.

"Once, in the evening — we hadn't gone to bed yet, Father and I, my mother had been dead for ages — we heard the clatter of horses' hooves and the rolling of wagon wheels stop outside our house, then the heavy thud of the knocker. My father took down his crutch, hobbled into the hallway to have a look, and after a while returned with a gentleman who to me no longer seemed young but was still very lively and had the most powerful eyes. The stranger produced a writ from our count to the effect that the holder thereof shall be permitted at any time and at his convenience to be shown all rooms of the house and have his every wish indulged. My father read the document out loud, then the stranger tucked it away. Father then asked the stranger if he'd rather not spend the night over at the post-office inn, where the driver was headed with his carriage and horses, because at this hour we surely couldn't offer him any convenience. In the morning he could see all he wanted, though he shouldn't expect to find anything out of the ordinary, no treasures or valuable works of art. No, the stranger explained, he wanted to tour the house right away and carefully inspect each room, because once the horses were rested he had to return first thing to Teplitz. Not for a moment could he be detained unnecessarily. High-level commitments and lofty affairs were awaiting him there. It hadn't been easy to get away even just for a couple of hours. He had raced here at breakneck speed, changing horses four times, entirely contrary to his usual manner and paying no heed to the scenery along the way. Indeed, his presence in this city seemed so unreal to him, more like a dream, something quite incredible, almost like a mirage, the intensification of an ardent wish that you're willing to accept as fact. Such moments were so rare you didn't even dare to try to make them last.

"Despite this insistence bordering on impetuousness, my father tried to persuade the visitor to stay just a little longer. 'Wouldn't your Excellency care to devote his attention to the city, the ancient astronomical clock on the Old Town Hall, the imperial and royal tombs in the cathedral, the bridge with its towers, the palaces?'

"'Thank you,' the stranger interrupted, 'but I know a good deal about this city. And we'll have to content ourselves with that for now. I was given an illuminating introduction by way of the local bookseller Calve, and I know from illustration and description the eminent majesty of this truly royal and ancient town which, quite irresponsibly, I have not yet been able to visit despite the repeated reminders of many a local friend. But now let's examine by candlelight those things that do not belong to the day.'

"I was able to infer that this distinguished stranger, referred to as his Excellency in the Count's letter but not introduced by name, knew a fair amount about the House of the Nine Devils. My father immediately prepared a lantern, I furnished myself with a wax candle, and we began our tour of the rooms that now seemed doubly spooky in the dark, with their squeaking floorboards, crackling walls, creaking chairs, here and there a scurrying mouse, the buckets, retorts and trivets strangely stirring and active under flickering, shifting light, as if they were once again in use, the balloon flasks shimmering and gleaming, dimly phosphorescing and real, as if the last remnants of something spectral were still floating around inside them. The visitor looked long and eagerly into these vitreous worlds, and it pleased me to watch him look at them. For his gaze was no astonished stare, it had a certain rhythmic flow, he didn't merely scan things with the eye but radiantly embraced them, a sudden recognition of something long since understood. I noticed this despite the fact that he sometimes looked in my direction. He picked up one of the balloon flasks and held it out in front of him on the tips of three fingers, even though the object must have been quite heavy. He tossed it lightly into the air, where it hovered for a brief second like a giant soap bubble before settling, leisurely and weightless, back into his outspread fingers. 'Did you notice the lively glow in the middle?' he asked. 'That comes from its levitating.' On a hanging shelf he set the celestial globe in motion. Then he turned the crank of the coelo-tellurion, I had to play the sun with my candlelight, and so the universe began to revolve. 'Now let's do a lunar eclipse!' he cried. 'Tycho might have done so with this very machine — it's old enough.' Thus he demonstrated the workings of the heavens. Never did a sun shine as splendidly as his words, and never again did a moon illuminate me as surely and gently as his gaze.

"Then we went down to the cellars. He picked up everything, examined the crucibles, mortars and pestles, the cauldrons and trivets to see if they still contained the remnants of former ideas, as he put it. He found things we didn't even know existed, oddities we'd never noticed before, brought objects back to life by means of quick comparisons. Bars of metal stacked in a corner he referred to as gold that had yet to be unriddled. He was like a young man, completely rejuvenated by these magic instruments, and I couldn't take my eyes off him. I was always right there behind him with my light. My father would eventually catch up with his crutch.

"In the lowest floor of the cellar there's a man-high iron door, just three hand lengths wide but heavy, with no lock, handle or bolt. What was behind it or where it led — we didn't know, because with every attempt to squeeze through the narrow gap, or even just shine a light inside, the flame would extinguish. But the visitor wanted to know what this door was for. It certainly had its quirks. It was sometimes easy to open or, rather, it was usually ajar. But whenever you pulled it open, no light would pass the threshold, seemingly obstructed by an invisible wall, so you didn't know what lay behind it: a room, a stairway or an abyss. No one ever dared to step through. 'It's a higher mystery,' the visitor said. 'Let's try to push back the inexplicable to its utmost limit.' He took a step into the placeless dark where no ray of light could reach him, the door closed with a screech, and my father and I stood before it in horror. We yelled, we pounded, we tried with all our might to loosen the heavy iron lid. But this time it wouldn't budge. No sound could be heard from the other side. My father went to fetch a crowbar and other tools, but, alas, to no avail. I fell to my knees and began to pray — to God, to the Infant Jesus of Prague, to the Black Madonna. But no one answered my prayers.

"Meanwhile morning had broken, and my father sent me to the post-office inn to ask about the driver and bring the blacksmith. The innkeeper shook his head. A driver with carriage and horses? He would have noticed that. No one stopped here, no carriage with a team of horses, not even a lone itinerant journeyman. That's impossible, I said. It's possible, the innkeeper said, that such a young lady would think it's impossible.

"But in times like those the impossible was indeed possible. And if there had been a driver with carriage and horses then he must have stopped somewhere else — that is, if he hadn't been swallowed up by the earth. I told the innkeeper and blacksmith about our nocturnal visitor and begged them to help us open the iron door as soon as humanly possible. The innkeeper didn't want to get involved. The blacksmith, though, who'd always been fond of me, proved willing, and came to the house with iron bars and wedges. But no sooner had we entered than my father greeted us with the words, 'It's done. The door opened on its own. But there's nothing behind it. You can't hear a soul.' The blacksmith went downstairs anyway, just to see for himself. He poked around in the darkness with his iron bars, but all he found there was emptiness. Pale-faced, he finally abandoned his efforts.

"There was no trace of our nocturnal visitor. No one had seen him or his carriage, and it wasn't long before everyone thought it was all a figment of my imagination, if not an extravagant lie which we used to give ourselves airs in front of others, who, as the war reached its turning point, had other, more important things on their minds. For our part we remained convinced that the visitor had disappeared through the cellar door and perished in the unknown. My father sent a report to the Count describing what had happened, and the Count even came in person to inspect the scene of the incident, though he surely didn't believe a word of what he'd read in the report. He considered it a deranged fantasy, the kind that leading a life in seclusion could easily give rise to. The fact that he had never given anyone permission to inspect our house was just one more proof of this. A document like this, especially without the name of its bearer, could only be a forgery. And if that were the case, the forger had received his just deserts. The Count even wanted to move us both to one of his country estates where the air was fresher and the surroundings more cheerful. But Father, who over the years had grown accustomed to the House of the

Nine Devils, would hear nothing of it. And so we stayed put, and gradually got used to the notion that our nocturnal visitor had gone from one indefinite reality to an even more indefinite one, indeed, that he had probably been a mere dream vision. And so the years passed by, as they are wont to do.

"Then one day, ten summers later — I was now a grown-up — my father handed me a sealed parcel. A post-boy had left it for me, he said. This was a major event, which is why I remember the year it happened: eighteen hundred and twenty-three. It was thrilling, because never before had anyone sent me anything. I was not the kind of person people sent things to. But the little package contained the oval portrait that's standing here right next to me. A portrait of the guest who disappeared. It arrived without a sender's address, and without a word of explanation. I asked the postmaster, but he was clueless. A parcel? He never delivered one to me. It was Father's word against the postmaster's, and I believed my father. Because obviously the portrait was there — a perfect likeness, old and young at the same time, with those big, unforgettable eyes. I can't say why I took the portrait down to the cellar, why I knelt down before the iron door, and why I propped it up against the doorframe. The light of my candle lit it up and I prayed for the lost man, as if doing so would somehow call him back — from the unentered, the unenterable. Suddenly the flame tilted, the door moved, and between the door and the iron frame the portrait silently slipped into the darkness, the very darkness that had once enveloped the visitor it depicted.

"I fell into a swoon and my father brought me upstairs. Since then I've never again set foot in the cellar. But you, not long after you came to our house, you recovered the portrait and thus restored me to life."

I was huddled up in a corner of the sofa while my father related this uncanny story. As bizarre as all of this sounded, I had two things to go on that suggested the story was genuine: the portrait and the iron door, which I'd seen with my very own eyes. "But how did you find the picture, Father?"

"Easy. Just days after moving in, I stumbled upon the iron door in the cellar while snooping around the old house. As usual, the door was slightly ajar. But something golden shimmered from the opening — the frame of the portrait, which I reached for without even knowing what it was. At the time I didn't know anything about this door's rather spooky qualities. But as I looked at the portrait in the light of my tallow candle the door slowly fell shut — and no one has managed to open it since."

"And why'd the old lady say you restored her to life by giving her the picture back?"

"That's easy to explain. First of all, she wasn't sure anymore if the visitor and, later, the portrait were real or if she'd only dreamed them. In the end she grew uncertain if she herself was even real. That's the kind of thing that happens in houses and cities like this. Her life was basically slipping through her fingers. When I brought her the portrait she could finally place it next to her, look at it and talk to it. It restored her sense of reality and with it her life."

But I was a skeptical boy, and — like every child, by the way — a relentless cross-examiner. "Do you think," I asked, "that the picture really depicted that man? Don't you think her father just found it somewhere and wanted to surprise her with it? Or maybe when you brought her the picture the old lady invented it all on a whim? Or maybe it was even you yourself who . . ."

"Enough!" my father interrupted, "Your thoughts are getting ahead of you. Why don't you go play ball instead and someday work for the railroad like me. Then you can ride the trains for free, to anywhere in the world — this one and the next."

My cousin Josef was an elementary teacher in the village of Neuzettel. The village had a population of five hundred and was located at the foot of Bramberg mountain, an hour's walk from Altzettel, which was twice as big and looked much more modern despite the "old" in its name. Indeed, Altzettel had developed, whereas Neuzettel, the more recent settlement, always considered itself sufficiently "new." Neuzettel and Altzettel were surrounded by fields and forests, and the shadow of Bramberg with its castle ruins fell at different times of the day on each of the two villages: on Neuzettel in the morning, on Altzettel in the afternoon.

Cousin Josef was generally referred to as a jack-of-all-trades. For apart from being a teacher he was also a carpenter, turner, potter, weaver, fiddler, zither-player, flutist and mechanic. Not only had he made the matrimonial beds himself, he was also skilled at intarsia and built the most abstruse apparatuses, including a perpetual-motion machine. The latter consisted of a large wheel on which individual glass tubes were mounted at equal distances so that when the wheel was set in motion fine-grained sand would pour from one tube into the next, thus driving the wheel and keeping it in motion. Of course the machine would stop before long. It took up half his workshop shed and, considering that he tinkered with it for years, it really was perpetual. In any event, it was in Cousin Josef's character to seek out things that were constantly in motion rather than the steadfast and constant. Cousin Josef's violin was, so he claimed, a genuine Cremona built by Antonio Amati. His reputation as a jack-of-all-trades was also due to his being well-informed about what went on in the world and having an answer for just about everything. Though he liked to drink beer, and quite a lot of it, and was sometimes even a little bit tipsy when he came into the classroom in the morning, he was never really drunk or even the slightest bit muddleheaded. Never in any of his many undertakings was he impaired by the effects of alcohol; instead, it tended to animate him and put a spring in his step.

One summer, after my last year of elementary school, I was sent to Neuzettel during vacation to stay with Cousin Josef. At that age summer break was sheer endless, lasting as it did from mid-July to mid-September. There were no obligations, not a care in the world, and my freedom was unlimited in Cousin Josef's house. He had only recently married. His wife was named Magdalena, or Lina for short, the daughter of a wealthy miller, somewhat languid in her movements, as is the wont of millers and their kin. (They certainly didn't learn it from the millstream.) Lina's house was therefore marked by a certain degree of pleasant disarray. You never knew which room you were in: the kitchen, living room, or the bedroom — a state of affairs that any young boy would find appealing.

The village community was made up of small farmers, some of whom practiced a trade on the side: one had an inn with a butcher shop, one was a cobbler, one was a tailor and a gravedigger into the bargain, one was a carpenter. The most impressive sideline was that of the blacksmith and horseshoer, and his was also one of the most important, since back in those days no one in Neuzettel had ever laid eyes on an automobile. Just above the village, close to the forest, was a so-called castle. There was nothing grandiose about it, just a somewhat longish two-story building with a mansard attic, surrounded by a walled-in garden. No one seemed to live in this castle, at least I never saw anyone going in or out of its iron-barred gate. All I managed to find out was that it belonged to some baronial family by the name of von Zettelsdorf. Neuzettel had no church. Sunday Mass was attended in Altzettel.

Cousin Josef had friends and enemies, as befits a "real" man. The blacksmith and the carpenter looked with disapproval on his mechanical and wood-working pursuits. I, too, was given a taste of this once when, watching the blacksmith at work one day, he drove me away with a gruffness that could not have been solely related to my harmless role as an onlooker. And once at the inn (Cousin Josef sometimes took me along), I heard the carpenter saying: "Here comes the jack-of-all-trades again," and I found his tone of voice obnoxious to say the least.

The inn had a gramophone with a giant amplifier made of battered sheet brass that sometimes emitted the crackling strains of "Happy are the days of youth, those days will never return." You could also hear the "Radetzky March," as well as a song about the future wonders of technology that went:

One day we will fly in balloons, that's for sure,
Five groschen, Vienna to Paris, grand tour.
And should pesky creditors get in your hair,
Then just tip your hat and be gone in the air.

"What does 'creditor' mean?" I asked Cousin Josef, to which he replied rather cryptically: "A creditor brings discredit." I should note that Lina preferred the fourth song on the inn's gramophone, "The sofa is my one real pleasure."

During vacation the whole village became my plaything: the dogs and their sniffing, the prowling cats, the geese at the village pond, the cows, pigs and horses — in short, all creatures great and small served to entertain me. Finding playmates among the village children was another matter. They formed a world of their own, with other habits and interests, with games unknown to me, with special duties and obligations. They spoke the Egerland dialect, which I didn't always understand, since in Prague, where I came from, one spoke the High German that was used in the chancellery of Holy Roman Emperor Charles IV. What's more, the village children showed a certain reserve toward city boys, which sometimes took the form of scorn. They would thumb their noses at me and stick out their tongues, followed by the occasional scuffle, in which I seldom came out on top.

From the earliest days of my youth, people and things were rarely just there for me to look at; I always wanted to be an active part of their lives and their doings. If they meant something to me, I wanted to mean something to them, too. Indifference to these efforts of mine gave me the feeling of dejection, loneliness and abandonment. But the violation of anything or anyone I considered my ally provoked my immediate retaliation, passionate, infinite retaliation, stopping at nothing, even if it meant self-injury.

For all my lack of playmates, I greatly enjoyed my time in Neuzettel. Each day for two minutes I set the perpetuum mobile in motion or climbed around in the attic with its paradise of chaos and junk, rummaging through crates of ancient books and magazines inherited from somewhere or other, the oldest of these being *Athenaeum,* the journal of the Romantics, which is why it was hanging sheet by sheet from a nail in the outhouse now, being used in a manner more in keeping with the times. Considerable stacks of the monthly put out by the Bohemian Museum (whose honorary members included the likes of Johann Wolfgang von Goethe) also served in this capacity, providing a sheer unlimited supply. Much of my formative education is thanks to this place of seclusion. So much for cultural life in the village.

I also began to work with my hands. From thin little black and white strips of wood I cut the square fields for an inlaid chessboard while Cousin Josef worked the lathe, artfully turning the figures for it. Even as a young boy I was very keen on chess, there having been a world chess champion, the first ever and maybe the greatest, in the family of my late mother. I'd learned to play chess with my father when I was barely six years old, helping him while away the many lonely Sundays and evenings of his widowerhood. Cousin Josef, who already owned a beautiful chess set, was working on the new one with me, for no other reason than to make a one-of-a-kind, one that was utterly special and unique. He had tried to teach his pretty Lina to play — to no avail, because after the first five moves she began to grow sluggish, as millers do, and unfailingly fell asleep before long. In me, on the other hand, he found an impassioned partner, roughly as good as he was. And so, in this respect, I was no longer merely a child but could hold my own against an adult and sometimes even win.

I was a boy in every other respect, doing boyish things, sometimes harmless, sometimes not so harmless, even careless or crude. I shot, for example, out the window with a shotgun, aiming at the sparrows in the cherry tree — not, of course, because I had it in for these poor unfortunate creatures, but because I took pleasure in action at a distance, like "far-shooting" Apollo, which even in the childlike days of myth was considered a magical and terrifying privilege reserved for the supreme Olympian god. It would be a mistake to assume I didn't love animals. I could spend an entire hour carefully trying to guide to freedom a sparrow that had gotten trapped in the attic. I took slugs and caterpillars from the hard country road and gently laid them aside in the grass. And all my life I've disliked the sight of cut flowers in vases, since to me they represented a high-handed act of violence against the order of nature and hence the sacred growth of plants, no less reprehensible than my puerile shooting of sparrows — which incidentally was soon to pass, depleting for the rest of my days all vestiges of an aggressive hunting instinct aimed at living creatures.

Having spent a few weeks in Neuzettel and its world, I had grown accustomed to skirting its fields, had explored its woods and thickets, hunted for mushrooms and picked blackberries, had encountered nutcrackers, partridges and hares, and even the occasional deer, knew the smell of a brewing storm and the clear, crystalline sounds of summer, could distinguish between the calls of peasants, and was familiar with the village down to its every nook and cranny, when one day I was out playing ball alone against the wall of the castle that belonged to the von Zettelsdorfs. The wall was my opponent and compliantly chucked the ball back, until suddenly one of my throws missed and the ball went flying right over it and into the garden on the other side. Naturally I lost no time climbing over the wall in order to fetch my ball. I have the suspicion the ball didn't fly into the garden by chance, that I had simply been looking for a reason to take a gander at these apparently inaccessible, silent, secret and, as it were, forbidden grounds.

What I saw at first were not well-tended beds but an overgrown tangle of plants that I had to fight my way through, then an unmown patch of grass with a confusion of wildflowers, a jumble of larkspur, catchfly and pasque-flower, as if I were in a forest meadow. At one particular spot I noticed something like an unkempt footpath, which I ventured to follow until suddenly I came to a sharp turn and was standing before a bench on which an old lady was sitting.

"How did you get in here," asked the lady, "and what do you want?"

She may have actually not been very old at all. It's possible she was only thirty, forty years old at the most. But she sat there as if she were old. Her question sounded firm, though not particularly harsh or terrifying. I only felt partly at fault, for I'd just been trying to recover my property.

"I'm looking for my ball," I said.

"So, you're looking for you ball. Well then, I'll help you look, and soon we'll see if you're telling the truth."

She got up, and I had to take her to the approximate spot where the ball had flown over the wall. We began to comb the tangle of plants and, although we did so thoroughly, which cost us a lot of time, our search was ultimately fruitless.

"I don't see any ball," the lady finally concluded.

"It must be hidden somewhere," I said, embarrassed and a little bit scared of being taken for a liar after all. "It really did fly over the wall," I insisted.

"I'd like to believe you," said the lady. "Come into the house with me. I'll find you another ball."

This was starting to get adventurous. Never in my life had I been in a castle. Castles, I knew from books, had something spooky about them. There might be trapdoors, or secret staircases, dungeons, torture chambers with an "iron maiden," suits of armor whose arms might unexpectedly come crashing down on your shoulders, ghosts that roamed the long hallways at midnight, sighing. Only it wasn't midnight, but a radiant summer afternoon. And anyway, the supposed spookiness of the place was just as enticing as it was unsettling. I also couldn't think of a good excuse to refuse the lady's request, which had sounded more like an order. So I followed her down the unkempt footpath until we reached the house.

She opened the creaking, iron-bossed door and led me through a spacious room in which an open grand piano stood, whose keyboard she struck in passing, sounding a brief chord that was faint and force-ful at once, and highly melodious, as if she'd wanted to make a friendly, casual remark; then she went up the stairs with me, into a room with a big bed and chest of drawers, whose lowest drawer she opened and began to rummage through. First she pulled out a small box of old photographs, which she looked at one by one and then began to put in order. Then she pulled out some children's toys: a doll that was missing a leg, a top, a little pair of ice-skates, a jumping rope and other girlish things, until finally she found a tennis ball which still had traces of the manufacturer's name printed on it.

"There's your ball," she said.

I thanked her. We went back down to the spacious room and I thought she would bid me farewell now. Instead she looked at me thoughtfully for a moment then said: "Sit down and listen."

I obeyed, thinking she was about to tell me some story or other, or maybe have me run an errand, but instead she sat down at the piano, diagonally across from me. I could see her face and hands, even her entire figure. Her face grew much more earnest than it had been already. Her hands hovered motionless over the keys momentarily. Her body grew tense, as if she were about to pounce on something. Then, unexpectedly, she began to play.

I didn't know and still don't know what she played, whether it was the work of some composer or her own fanciful creation. All I know is that what emanated from that piano and filled the room was she her-self, it was indivisible from her and included everything around her: the shapes and gestures of the furniture, the play of colors of the pic-tures on the wall, my very own self, which was soon nothing more than a part of these sounds, which her gaze, her quietly swaying body, her hands roaming up and down the keyboard, her gently vibrating fingers communicated to this instrument by way of an agitated band of black and white. My listening was a total negation of gravity, a sweet loss of physical sensation, a transition into a new aggregate, the dissolution of soft and loud, into a world of unearthly relationships and figures, devoid of place, much less of time.

Then, once again, I found myself in the midst of silence. The lady, too, sat motionless in her silence, as if she were just a painting like the other works of art around her. Then she said:

"Go now. And come back the same time tomorrow. But don't be coming and going through the garden gate. Climb over the wall."

She saw me to the door.

"Promise me you won't tell anyone you were here."

I held her hand and solemnly swore, and with the other she gently caressed me on the temple. Then I ran back to the tangle of plants where I'd jumped into the garden, climbed back over the wall, and stole in the setting sun to Cousin Josef's house.

Lina had prepared noodle soup for dinner, with a few blackish slices of birch bolete floating on the surface, the consumption of which was followed by a discussion about whether yellow birch boletes were preferable to orange ones or whether as soup mushrooms slippery jacks, known in these parts as *klouzky,* weren't the better choice. This was followed by *Totsch,* a deep-fried pancake made of raw grated potatoes mixed with soured milk, a crusty, thirst-inducing dish. Lina then cleared the table and leisurely took up her knitting gear to work on a pointy cap, seeing as a baby was on the way. Cousin Josef unfolded his paper, a staunchly conservative "Czech-eating" organ that bore the name *The Watch on the Mies.* After reading a while he turned to his wife and asked:

"You want to come along to Pfannerer's?"

He didn't say: Shall we go to Pfannerer's, but was clearly expressing that *he* was going either way and that Lina had the choice of coming along or staying home. Pfannerer's was an inn named after its owner and whose sign read: "Emil Pfannerer's Guesthouse and Meat Market."

Lina understood that the offer was made on condition that she turn it down. She yawned profusely and finally declared that, no, she did not want to come along to Pfannerer's. Whereupon Cousin Josef grabbed his hat and cane and prepared to go alone.

"Take a beer glass with you," said Lina.

Now, Pfannerer's had beer glasses aplenty. It was prudent, however, to bring your own since on the way back home you could put a candle in it and use it as a lantern, which came in handy in the pitch-black of night on extremely bumpy village roads, not to mention if you were in a drunken stupor. Cousin Josef took the recommended precautions and left.

I remained sitting in the window niche, where the light of the kerosene lamp couldn't reach me, doing nothing at all. Lina knitted away mechanically, only now and then interrupting her silence to engage in a prolonged yawn that ran through every note of the scale, either up or down. Under normal circumstances I would have found the situation a little dreary. This time I was happy, though, sitting in the semi-darkness and not having to speak to anyone.

I thought of the lady. I was familiar with the term from chess, the "lady" being the queen in German: mightiest mistress of every square on the board, the most noble and beautiful of all the figures, the most mature as well, no girl, no child. A real lady, in other words, calling all the shots, a queen with pawns, rooks and knights as well as bishops in her service, even the king himself in his baby-step submissiveness, his very survival crucially dependent on everything she does or doesn't do. With a naturalness that behooved only her she had drawn me into the strangeness of her being and with me erected a secret against the world, thus conceding to me a fractional amount of power in her life.

I slept very little that night. The next morning I made an attempt to continue cutting the squares of the chessboard, but it wasn't really working so I left well alone. So as not to be there at lunchtime I said I was going on an outing to the ruins of Bramberg castle. I hiked through the countryside, up the mountain, between juniper bushes and granite blocks, thinking only of that hour that promised to repeat the experience of the previous day. From the top of the mountain I looked out over the ruined walls toward the forests of Bavaria, saw below me the threads of smoke rising from the chimneys of Neuzettel, discerned the elongated shape of the castle with its magical garden: my countryside, my father's countryside, the lady's countryside, God's country like every country, but its meaning for me was deeper now.

Neuzettel lay in the afternoon sun when, at the same hidden spot as the day before, I climbed over the castle wall, jumped into the maze of plants, and took the path to her house. No one was in the garden. I was utterly at ease, for I knew I had rights of hospitality. Out of sheer impatience I forgot to even knock but simply unlatched the door and entered the big room, whose curtains were drawn so that my eyes first had to adjust to the semi-darkness.

"You're punctual," she observed. She gestured to a table with a plate of cherries on it and said: "Eat first."

It occurred to me that I didn't even know the lady's name. She hadn't asked for mine either. Women in castles had beautiful names. Viktoria, Isabella, or suchlike.

"Maybe later," I said, not helping myself to the cherries.

She merely nodded, and without another glance in my direction sat down at the grand piano. Her hands made a few brief runs up and down the keyboard, as if first she wanted to come to some agreement, conversing with the tones about the impending piece. Then she paused, and her bearing suddenly acquired an evocative radiance, so that everything in the room from now on seemed obedient to her, seemed to be at her mercy. A single, muted tone arose from an infinite distance, called forth other tones and flowed up like a vigorous stream that suddenly collected against the darkly rising weir of hammered strings, swelled and widened before crashing down over the weir, rushing onward forcefully, impulsively. I heard hills, trees and forests rising up all around and encircling the waters, which continued to speak in regular, tranquil rhythms. Stags belled, while echoes issued from the tributary valleys. The sun was high. The water glittered. Fish rose to the surface and sank to the depths like oblong silver leaves. Then, from the clear cool torrent, a hand rose up, held fast to the roots of the alders at the water's edge, and gradually drew up a bright glistening body behind it. In glorious freedom she lifted herself to the banks like marble, her outstretched arms wondrously exposed. I stood on the other side and only saw the open radiance, the gentle cosmos of floating worlds, the stars of her gaze and the soft, mysterious, cloudy depths. She slowly turned, a ray of light caressed her silhouette and her shadow extended across the water, touching me. I trembled, and she vanished.

"Once upon a time," said the lady, "yes, once upon a time I was beautiful. But you wouldn't understand that."

"You're *very* beautiful. More beautiful than anything."

She smiled.

"Enough for today," she said. "You may come again tomorrow. But now eat some cherries."

She sat down and ate with me.

"You eating, I wouldn't have thought!" I said, astonished.

"Don't talk now," she retorted.

She led me silently through several rooms. The furnishings seemed ancient and dusty, but well-arranged. A large painting hung in the last room. It depicted a girl, a child still, with blue ribbons in her hair and a jumping rope in her hands, about to hop through it.

"It's a good likeness," she said.

I marveled that she, too, had once been a child.

She accompanied me to the garden wall. She stood there, noble, in the garden's fair weeds, her wordless wave, a seamless gesture, beckoning me over the wall.

In the evening, Lina pulled out her family album. It was bound in brown pressed leather and was actually a music box. The cover was embossed with a depiction of the Trumpeter of Säckingen. If you opened the album, the melody "Life is a loathsome affair" would play, in curious contrast to the wedding photos. My stepmother had chosen this witty chime as a morning-gift for the newlyweds. She had brought a similar dowry into her marriage, its cover displaying the two-tailed Bohemian lion, and when opened it played the melody of the following Czech folksong:

> Sleep, Havlíček, it won't be long,
> Our nation merrily
> Sings your song
> Sleep in everlasting light!
> Fearless Czech, the German he will fight.

Whenever the album was opened, my German-minded father went livid with rage and the inevitable political quarrel that ensued would sometimes culminate with the shattering of porcelain plates.

The lamentations of the Trumpeter of Säckingen did not cause any conflict between the young married couple, but melodies of any kind now cut me to the quick. So when Cousin Josef began to play *Stephanie Gavotte* on his violin I tried to slip away unnoticed.

"Why do you wanna go out in the dark?" he asked.

"Oh, no particular reason. Just to see the stars."

"There are no stars. It's going to rain."

"I'm not afraid of the rain."

It was raining, soft and gentle. But I really didn't mind. There is no bad weather in the countryside, because every kind of weather is a perfect part of nature. The rain did me good. I enjoyed stepping in the puddles and relished the feeling of raindrops on my skin. The lights were still on at Pfannerer's. The gramophone proclaimed: "Happy are the days of youth! Those days will never return." Otherwise all was quiet in the village. The only thing to be heard was the rain's conversation in the lime trees and the gutters, and the quiet murmur of the cloak of water spilling over the darkness.

The rain had stopped by morning, but the clouds were still there. The village yawned in its grayness. I was in the workshop early. I gave the perpetuum mobile a shove, and it creaked.

"It has to be oiled now and then," said Cousin Josef.

Then I went up to the lathe.

"What do you think you're doing? Be careful. You have to learn how to work a lathe."

"Let me try."

"What do you want to make?"

"A chess piece. Maybe a queen."

"Well then, pay attention. I'll show you how it's done."

"But I want to do it myself."

"What's the matter with you? You can't just do it on a whim, it doesn't work that way."

He took a maple rod, inserted it, stepped on the treadle and with the chisels began to work the rotating dowel. The base assumed its rounded form, and then the gently vibrating body began to swell in the middle.

"Now comes the neck and the collar. You have to be careful with this part."

The spindle was whirring, and the different edges of the chisel faintly sounded in varying pitches.

"Sounds like music, doesn't it? Now comes the head. This is the hardest part."

"Let me try."

"Okay, if you insist."

I took the chisel and set to work. The head broke off.

"You see? I told you. It takes experience and a steady hand."

The day advanced, slowly and deliberately. After lunch I headed toward the edge of the woods. Entire families of yellow chanterelles had shot up after the rain from the needles on the ground. A woodpecker worked away at a tree trunk. Tiny pearls of water glistened here and there on the little veils of cobweb stretching over the mosses.

I skirted the village until I came to the castle wall. Climbing over, I slipped and fell into the damp garden undergrowth. I scrambled to my feet and went to the house. The boggy ground squished underfoot.

It was almost completely dark in the spacious room. The sky outside was overcast, and virtually no light at all came in through the closed curtains.

"Sit down. You know your spot."

I groped my way forward and waited. I saw the lady, my queen, indistinctly. After a while she began to play.

A couple of precipitous chords rose up like a group of basalt columns, looming in solitude. They grew ever fainter, smaller and smaller in vanishing monotony, until they disappeared entirely. Now all that remained was a horizontal surface devoid of cardinal points, and within it the lady, a lone black vertical. No sign of living nature, no grass, no shrub was visible. All around her was nothing but rubble and rock. Some of the stones formed into crystals, into tiny prisms and pointed pyramids that would have been impossible to walk on. She, too, stood there motionless. Only for a few seconds did she flare up and glow, extinguishing just as soon into the blackness of her pose. It was terrible to hear these, as it were, motionless tones, the suspension of meaning. Monstrous pauses gaped between heartbeats. Then, in her stony realm, she slowly bowed and descended. She turned into crystal. I saw her sparkle one last time. Then a geode closed around her. All that remained was a mute desert.

"Now go and don't come back."

I stood up and heard her add faintly:

"You needn't climb the wall. Go through the garden gate."

The next day Cousin Josef said to Lina: "Did you know the castle lady was back again?"

"How should I know that? She comes and goes as she pleases, and no one knows when or why."

"Who's the castle lady?" I asked.

"She's the owner of the castle. Each year she comes for three days then disappears again."

"How come nobody notices when she comes? The village is a small place."

"She comes at night, never goes out, and leaves again at night. It all happens so unexpectedly."

It sounded like he was talking about a ghost.

"How do you know she was here?" I asked.

"You could see a light at night. And this morning the wheel tracks in the mud. The only one who knows for sure is old Schaubschläger. He always drives her. But you can't get a word out of him."

"So she is a real person?"

"What do you mean, a real person? She was born and raised here. But that was before my time. Only the older folks know much about her. And the only one who really knows her is old Schaubschläger, who used to be the castle gardener. Maybe twenty years ago or more."

Old Schaubschläger lived alone in his retirement cottage on the outskirts of the village. Behind it was a pasture adjacent to the woods. I hung around there a lot the next few days, but didn't catch sight of the old man. He had a horse that grazed in a paddock in the daytime, and in his shed a kind of landau, which he occasionally used for carting purposes.

Finally he came to the door.

"What do you think you're doing snooping around here, city boy," he asked, looking at me with ice-gray eyes.

"I'm just out for a walk. I like it here."

My answer didn't seem to convince him. He began to sharpen a scythe, the blows sounding deeper or higher-pitched, depending on whether he struck the wide or the narrow end. This went on for quite a while. Then he said:

"How's ol' Jack-of-all-trades? Still fiddling?"

"Yeah, he still plays."

"He says it's Italian, his violin. But I don't believe it, that's humbug."

"Why? There's a paper inside it. It says it's Italian. From the year 1630."

"It's not hard to stick a piece of paper somewhere."

"But it sounds so beautiful," I said.

Old Schaubschläger began to sharpen again and sank into contemplation.

"Sounds so beautiful," he said, and you didn't know if he was talking about the violin or the scythe. "That all depends on who's playing what," he finally added. "I've heard other kinds of music."

"What do you mean?"

"Like I'm going to tell you! Now get lost."

So I toddled off and was well on my way to the woods when he called out after me:

"Hey you," he said, "tell Jack-of-all-trades that if he wants to buy a piano he can get one cheap pretty soon."

Near the end of August there was a furniture auction in the castle garden. The house and property had gone to a new owner. The overgrown garden was full of people. They'd come from Altzettel, from Pfraumberg, from Plan, from Tepl, and even from Mies to take part in the sale. The house itself was off-limits. Trunks, tables, chairs, all kinds of gadgets and appliances, even a chest of drawers were set up outside the entrance, and an auctioneer offered them up for sale, going once, going twice, sold. I watched for a while then snuck around the garden, climbed up and over the wall and was gone.

When I got home in the evening, Josef and Lina were standing in the workshop admiring the piano Cousin Josef had bought for a pittance. They'd put it in the workshop for the time being, since this was attached to the house at ground level and was the biggest space they had.

"It's a Bösendorfer," said Cousin Josef proudly. "The castle lady always played it as a child. Then she didn't touch it anymore. And now she's not coming back, either."

"She never played it again, you say?"

"Nope, never. Not since her fiancé died in a hunting accident. That's what people say. It's a little bit out of tune, the ol' box. But that can be remedied. Piano tuning, that's my specialty."

He ran his fingers up and down the keys.

"Leave the piano alone," I shouted angrily.

"What's the matter with you? You've got a screw loose, or what?"

"Don't play it. If you do I'll run away, I'm going home."

"He's nuts," said Lina. "Delirious without a fever."

Cousin Josef lit up a cheroot.

"City kids are nothing but trouble. Every one of 'em a bundle of nerves," he said.

"He bolted during the Trumpeter of Säckingen, too," added Lina accusingly.

Later the three of us all went to Pfannerer's. Half the village was there, celebrating the auction. The "Radetzky March" was playing, along with the tune about the hot-air balloon, the days of youth that are gone forever, and the sofa you lie on to give yourself a treat. Pfannerer had bargained himself a sofa. They spoke about the new owner of the house and his plans to remodel it. An architect from Tepl had already been there and measured the place. The taproom was filled with tobacco smoke and the smell of beer. The auctioneer was also there, eating knockwurst with vinegar and onions.

"Our esteemed teacher really hit the jackpot with that piano," he said.

"That's right, a Bösendorfer. Just a little out of tune. The castle lady used to always play on it."

"A pity about the castle lady," said old Schaubschläger.

"Why's it a pity?" asked the blacksmith. "She was never there anyway, or just for a couple of days, like some kind of ghost."

"She was a beautiful woman," countered Schaubschläger.

"You talk like a real lady-killer," said the carpenter.

"Beautiful woman, ha!" said the blacksmith. "More like a witch."

"How would you know, you bum? You didn't even know 'er," said Schaubschläger, flaring up. "Say that one more time and I'll sock you one."

"Shush, will you! You're pathetic! You probably had something with her!" yelled the blacksmith.

At that moment something terrible happened to me. I only have a dim recollection of it. I felt myself get up and stagger to the table where the blacksmith was sitting just a few paces away. I stood before him and stared him straight in the eyes. He stared right back at me and said, uneasily: "What do *you* want?"

Then my hands balled up into fists, and suddenly — I don't know how it happened — one of my fists struck his full glass of beer, causing it to topple over and spill its brown liquid in one big gush across the table and onto the blacksmith.

For a second there was petrified silence in the tavern. I saw the blacksmith get up and raise his arm. Then everything went black.

As I slowly regained consciousness, in a corner under a bench, a raucous tavern brawl was underway. Everyone seemed to be trouncing everyone, profanities went whizzing back and forth, blows were raining left and right as if the number of people had increased tenfold. In the midst of this melee, the innkeeper cranked up the "Radetzky March," and, grotesque as it seems, I heard myself humming along to it, even crooning an old Prague version of the lyrics:

Radetzky, Radetzky he was pretty neat:
Gave spuds to the army, and kept
for himself all the meat,

until a well-aimed beer glass went crashing into the gramophone's trumpet and the melody was shattered. Then, all of a sudden, someone flung the door open and a shriek pierced the general hubbub: "Fire! Jack-of-all-trade's shed is burning!"

For a moment everyone froze in place, fists, beer glasses and chair legs raised. Then they began to walk and run, and before long I was alone in the taproom.

I trailed behind and, once outside, saw the workshop going up in flames. They yelled and shouted in every tone of voice. The village fire engine led the way, followed by the bucket brigade, pails flying from hand to hand from the pond. Cousin Josef ran up and down, and tried to get into the shed to salvage what he could. They had to hold him back by force.

"You're insured," I heard someone say.

"Not the piano," cried Josef. "And the violin, good God, my violin!"

"It's a fake anyway," shouted old Schaubschläger.

"Why do you say that? It's a Cremona," wailed Josef, "I bought it in Podersam, from my teacher."

"Stop your bickering and do something!" hollered the carpenter. But there wasn't much to be done. The fire blazed away mercilessly. The best they could do was keep it away from the house, aiming the water hose at the walls and the roof beams. The flames leapt out of the workshop windows, and now this object, now that one could be seen being burned to ashes. I saw the perpetual-motion machine as it began to spin furiously then fly to pieces. I saw the piano lid warp and buckle, and it seemed that the flaming instrument was emitting frenetic chords before it burned to the ground and vanished. Meanwhile I'd regained my senses and no longer felt any pain. Instead of making myself useful, though, I huddled motionless in a dark clump of bushes and watched. By dawn all that was left of the workshop was a couple of smoldering beams and charred foundation walls. The house remained undamaged.

The authorities came in the morning, the constables from Altzettel and a man from the insurance company. They tried to determine the cause of the fire, but no one had a clue. Everyone had either been at the inn or at home in bed when the fire broke out.

No one asked me.

Had they done so I might have told them about a spark of destruction that had jumped from my soul into the old grand piano, about a smoldering fire in the depths that had no choice but to erupt, so that what had ended could complete its destiny in a grand and noble manner, and so the beautiful didn't perish in the absurdity of the vulgar and ordinary. But how could I, a mere boy, have known how to say and explain all this, and who would have understood?

A few days later, Cousin Josef brought me to the station in Altzettel. From the short train platform you could see Bramberg mountain with its ruins in the clarity of a late summer, the blue-black spruce forest on the slope, and the fields already harvested. It was the last time I saw Cousin Josef.

"A pity," he said upon parting, "we never finished making that chessboard. And I never played on the piano either. Didn't even get to tune it. But why am I telling *you*? You're not musical anyway."

NEW YEAR'S COMMOTION

The boy trudged through the suburban street. Laboriously he worked his way forward, the soft snow nearly reached his shoe tops and hadn't stopped falling yet. It was freezing cold and two in the morning. Why does a twelve-year-old boy struggle alone through swirling snow, so late at night in poorly lit, deserted streets, searching the sidewalk for something? I know, because it was me.

To make matters worse, he had a sore throat. But the boy didn't tell his father, because then he would have had to stay home. His father wasn't able to go himself. First of all he'd been drinking, it being New Year's Eve; second, his gallbladder was acting up; third, whenever there was a problem like the one with his wallet he was rendered helpless and nearly broke down and cried; fourth, and this was the most important thing, the boy really wanted to go himself, not just to be useful and prove what he was capable of, but because the snow was calling him, as was the night, this special night he had heard so much about for many years now. He also had to go because he was a little scared of going and wanted to overcome his fear. It's astonishing how many things have to come together for a twelve-year-old boy in shorts, with a flimsy coat and a sore throat, to be allowed to walk in the driving snow at two in the morning on New Year's Eve through a suburb of Prague illuminated only by dim gas lanterns and reflections from the snow. A truly historical night — otherwise I wouldn't be talking about it almost fifty years later.

You didn't feel the cobblestones, for the snow was velvety and piling up fast, an aggravating circumstance that made searching harder. The wallet, so his father lamented, contained three hundred florins. Well, not a full three hundred, since some of it had stayed at the City of Moscow tavern or been spent on other entertainments during the course of this festive evening. But it was almost three hundred florins — his monthly salary, in other words, and a New Year's bonus of the same amount. An enormous sum of money! And now it was maybe lost forever. Opposed to this "maybe" and its dire consequences was the boy's resolve to scour the entire distance back to Seilergässchen, the side street where the aforementioned tavern was located. It was almost the same as his daily route to school, which took about half an hour and he knew like the back of his hand, every oriel, every gutter, every shop window along the way. His stepmother had been against his going, but she was opposed to everything, and that was just one reason more for him to stand by his decision, no matter how long he'd been lying snugly in bed after a cozy, lonely evening. He was content with being alone. He'd been reading by the light of the kerosene lamp. "Stand, traveler, and give the password, which will save thee from my weapon." Then he gargled some alum on account of the lump in his throat. He knew how to fend for himself. Then he fell asleep. And then his father and stepmother got home, laughing at first in the adjacent room, then pestering each other with questions, followed by an inexplicable toing and froing, then there was yelling and bickering and mutual recriminations because of the missing wallet, not to mention complaints about the gallbladder attack that inevitably accompanied such altercations. The boy knew one thing: Money was important. He'd once lost a florin while fetching some beer from the nearby Crown of Bohemia tavern. He came back with neither florin nor beer. The uproar was almost as big back then as this time with the three hundred. And the slaps in the face were something to remember.

Onward he trudged, scanning the sidewalk as he walked. The snow could have covered up the wallet by now, but maybe it was peeping out from underneath. The searching went so slowly that he needed almost fifteen minutes to get to what was known as "Bulgarian Corner," even though on his way to school this distance took him just four minutes. Arriving here, he noticed with dismay that an unexpected mishap had suddenly set him back. The house key! It was no longer in his coat pocket. With all the bending over it must have slipped through a hole in his pocket. It was the first time in his life he'd been entrusted with the house key. They paid the janitor an entire florin extra each month for the option of using the house key, and there was no telling what would happen if he lost it. He would have to ring the bell and wake up the janitor when he got back. And then there was his father to contend with, good Lord! A boy mustn't lose an important object if he's been entrusted with it. So he traced his way back, step by step, searching for the key in the snow. He was lucky and eventually found it, right next to a sewer grate. His hand snatched it up as if it might elude him the very last minute and slip irretrievably through the sewer grate. Getting sidetracked cost him another quarter of an hour. But the incident bolstered his confidence, for if the house key had been recovered the wallet might be too. The mounds of snow were actually quite delightful, but he couldn't think of things like snowmen in the midst of such an important mission. He would have loved to skid on the ice but he had to keep on looking, and this meant one step at a time.

The scene transformed when he got back to the tavern at Bulgarian Corner, where a broad street illuminated by arc lamps ended and where people were milling around, individually or in groups, hooting and howling, singing and shouting, exclaiming "Happy New Year." The boy couldn't pay much attention to them. He combed the sidewalk with its trampled snow. He knew that his father, on his way home from the City of Moscow, always walked on the side of the street next to the fence of the freight depot. He had walked this route with him plenty of times back when he was still very little and his stepmother wasn't yet in the house. He contemplated all the ways you could possibly lose a wallet, like reaching into one's pocket to grab a handkerchief or buying something from a hot-dog vendor, but there must have been an endless number of reasons for reaching into a coat pocket and dropping a wallet by accident during the general commotion of a night like New Year's Eve. Perhaps the wallet had been found already and the finder had become its keeper, or maybe he was an honest fellow who turned it in to the police. But even if someone is honest, who goes to the police on New Year's Eve? Honest finders are entitled to one-tenth of the value, the boy had once heard someone say. Surely there must be people who are willing to surrender nine-tenths for honesty's sake. But even the loss of even one-tenth would be a harsh blow to his father's budget.

The boy continued walking slowly, past the state railroad station until he got to the Powder Tower, then to the right along the Graben. Crossing the street opposite the Blue Star Hotel, he almost got run over by a fiacre that, luckily, was moving slow because of all the snow. But he had to search carefully when crossing the street, even more so than on the sidewalks, and couldn't well pay attention to passing vehicles too. No one paid attention to him before he got to the Graben. But on the Graben people seemed in high spirits and they frolicked, joked and hindered him. The snow was blowing from all directions, even from the ground, oddly enough, and stuck to his lashes as if it were trying to complicate his task. At one point he suddenly found himself in the midst of a tangle of pedestrians, it must have been an entire family, or several, laughing and screaming, a little girl, too. They all wore colorful paper hats, paper streamers hung on their coats which, apart from being covered with snowflakes, were strewn with tiny pieces of confetti. "Hey there, young man," they called out, "*prosit* — here's to the New Year!" while the girl flung a snowball right into his face. The snowball was a tonic. He was no slouch and lobbed a few back. The whole group now began hurling snowballs in all directions through the driving snow. It was fun. Everyone chased each other back and forth, and the boy chased the girl all the way into the Grand Bazaar arcade with its Gaea Panorama. It was closed now, of course, but the door displayed ads for next week's program: "Elephant hunt in Africa," "Life in a Dutch Windmill."

"Were you ever in the panorama?" he asked the girl. "Sure, hundreds of times," she said.

He'd only been there once himself. It cost a full five kreutzers for children. He held onto the girl by her arms. She resisted a while and then screamed: "Let me go or I'll tell my mother." But he didn't let go, and they struggled until she got away, finding refuge in a niche between two display cases, where there happened to be a mirror, in which she carefully regarded herself in the dim light of the arcade. He was right behind her, and now stood beside her in front of the mirror. He felt kind of shabby standing next to her, this pretty girl in a blue coat and little fur collar, with a pointed golden paper hat nestling in her curls.

"I got you," he yelled, and was about to grab her by the hand again. "No you don't" she cried, quickly turning away. Then she shrieked: "My earring! I've lost my earring, all because you were chasing me."

The boy was alarmed to have caused such a mishap. "What did it look like?" he asked.

"Just like the other one, you imbecile. Made of gold, with three little blue stones like a forget-me-not. I got them for my name day."

"What's your name?" he asked, as if by knowing her name he could find the earring better.

"Emma," she said.

They now began a desperate search in the poorly lit arcade. The adults the girl was with eventually caught up with them. "What are you two up to?" they called, and, "Having a good time?"

"No," the girl said, "I lost an earring because this boy was chasing me."

"You're a very naughty boy," said a woman, surely the mother, with a liberty cap made of paper on her head. "An earring, and a gold one to boot. The whole New Year's Eve wasn't worth losing that."

"Oh, come on," said a man from their group, "Don't lose your head. Emma could have broken a leg, you know."

"I've got it!" called out the boy. "It was there right under the panorama door."

"It's a good thing, you little tramp," said the mother. "Now get lost." And the whole group including the girl, who didn't so much as glance behind her, left through the arcade and continued to the Obstmarkt.

The boy watched them walk away and wondered which day was Emma's. Then he remembered why he'd gone out in the first place: to find his father's wallet. He went back to the Graben and continued through the throng of people, scanning the sidewalk as he went. He found something toward the end of the Graben, unfortunately not the wallet, but a small pocketknife nonetheless, with a mother-of-pearl handle. Only a careful seeker like the boy could have noticed it in the snow. He put it with the key, which he'd been careful this time to stow in a different pocket, one without a hole. He would probably have to turn in the pocketknife, even though it was the kind he'd always wanted. Not turning it in would be tantamount to lying, and "those who lie, cheat. Those who cheat, steal. Those who steal, end up on the gallows," according to his father. But his father said a lot of things.

From the end of the Graben, at Wenceslas Square, it was just a short walk to Seilergässchen. They called that spot Am Brückl, and the growing mass of passersby made searching particularly difficult there. Finally he stood across from the City of Moscow, where they were busy putting the chairs up on the tables. All the customers had left by now. The headwaiter, Herr Votruba, directed the clean-up work of the two underwaiters and the busboy. He looked surprised when he saw the boy, whom he knew from his father's visits.

"What do *you* want?" he asked. "Your esteemed parents are long gone, they left almost two hours ago."

"I know," said the boy, "but my father lost something."

"Is that so," said Votruba. "That can happen. What did he lose?"

"I have to look for it," the boy said evasively. He didn't reveal what he was looking for. Experience had taught him to be a little more cautious.

"He was sitting over there," said Votruba, pointing to the table reserved for the regulars, on top of which stood a black-red-gold collection box of the League of Germans in Bohemia with the inscription: "We Germans fear God, but nothing else in the world."

"And why didn't your Herr Papa come get it himself?" the headwaiter persisted.

"He's sick," said the boy.

"Sick? But all he ate was goulash soup and herring salad. Sick? People get sick pretty fast these days, I guess. Red today, dead tomorrow, said Napoleon when he lost the Battle of Aspern. Everyone loses something. Come here, I wanna tell you a story."

"I have to keep looking," said the boy.

Herr Votruba had surely partaken in his own little New Year's celebration after the last of the guests had departed and he seemed a little woozy. "Come here when I wanna tell you something," he said almost commandingly. "Cut the shenanigans. You can look all you want later. It won't run away from you."

Votruba commanded his respect, and, given the circumstances, the boy didn't want to upset him.

"Sit down," said Herr Votruba, "and listen up. I once lost something myself. My father sent me away to be apprenticed as a busboy and I ended up losing my suitcase. Changing trains in Böhmisch-Trübau. I'm from Moravia, you oughta know. I set my suitcase down on the platform, next to a dozen other ones. Along comes a lady, one of them with a giant hat and twenty bird's nests on it — 'Upstairs, ooh! Downstairs, pew!' as they say — and she says to me: 'Here's a six-kreutzer, hurry up and run to the station restaurant before the train arrives and get me a sausage with horseradish, but make sure it's packed to go.' There were no dining cars back then. So me, at the start of my busboy career, I run off straight across the tracks, but no sooner am I inside the restaurant than the train pulls in; the waitress is taking her time and starts asking me all kinds of questions: my name, where I'm from, and rubbish like that. I have to run to the last wagon, the horseradish sausage in my hand, and all the way around the long train, and when I finally look for my suitcase it's gone, along with all the others. Instead of just getting on the train, stupid me, ass that I am, runs back and forth like a maniac, finds the lady and hands her the sausage through the window. 'Thank you,' she says, as the train starts to move and I stand on the platform like Europe's fool. Can you imagine what it means for someone who's not even a busboy yet to stand without a suitcase on a platform in Böhmisch-Trübau? Well, at least I had my ticket. 'You can take the next train in five hours,' the stationmaster in the red cap tells me — you know what I'm talking about, your father's a railroad official. But what does a person do for five hours in Böhmisch-Trübau? It was still afternoon, so I walked into town, feeling pretty miserable. I had no money either, just enough to get started. So I wander around the streets for a while, not a whole lot to see there really, just on the town square, a Marian column with some steps in front of it. I sit down on the steps, where else was I supposed to sit? Along comes this stocky fellow, who asks me: 'What are you doing here, and what's your name? You're not from around here.' I tell him the truth: 'I'm an aspiring busboy, just passing through and have to wait for the next train.'

"'A busboy,' the man says, 'then stay right here, you can work for me as soon as you want.' He ran a place called the Concordia. I ended up staying ten years there."

"I have to keep looking," said the boy.

"Hold on," said Herr Votruba, "I haven't finished my story yet. So I stayed there ten years and even married the owner's daughter, who's still my wife to this day. But I never did see my suitcase again. There wasn't much inside it, just some underwear and a suit and an extra pair of boots and a dried sausage and sweet rolls, who knows who ate those, but still it hurt, 'cause my silver Confirmation watch was in it too. I got the owner's daughter, but the Concordia itself went to her older brother; there were constant quarrels with him, so eventually we moved away. Then I was a waiter in Budweis, and at Pilsen Station in Saaz. The Lord sure works in mysterious ways."

"Yes, sir," said the boy, hoping he could finally get down to searching.

"Hold on," said Votruba, "the best is yet to come. In Saaz I started working as an underwaiter. They live it up there with all the hops merchants. Nothing but fancy rich people. And already on my second day of work, at closing time, the headwaiter pulls his watch from his pocket and I can hardly believe my eyes: it's my Confirmation watch. 'Upon my soul, that's my watch,' I blurt out. 'What do you mean, your watch,' he hollers, 'seems to me your head's not screwed on right.' 'It's got my monogram on it, J.W.,' I say, 'and the number 2033 inside the double case.' The headwaiter pops open the back cover and sure enough the number's inside it. 'I bought it fifteen years ago in Prague from a secondhand dealer,' he says, and I tell him about how I lost my suitcase in Böhmisch-Trübau. We both nearly cried. Then he offers it to me at cost price, two florins fifty, but it's got yellow spots, 'cause it turns out it wasn't made of silver after all, but of silver-plated nickel. How could I not be sore at ol' Kulka, my Confirmation sponsor. By then he'd been dead for years, of course. But dead or not: The sun will bring it to light."

The boy waited to see if something else would follow. But Votruba seemed to be done with his story and the boy could now begin his search. He crawled around underneath the tables, combed the corners and, just to be on the safe side, even went out to the urinals, but didn't find a thing.

"What should I do now, Herr Votruba?" he asked a little hoarsely, for the sore throat he'd nearly forgotten began to make itself felt again.

"Indeed, what should we do? You still haven't told me what you're looking for."

"The wallet," said the boy this time. "Maybe someone found it."

"If someone had found it they would have turned it in," said Votruba, slightly offended. "Anyway, none of the waiters found it. None of the regulars either. As far as the other customers are concerned, none of them were still around by the time your esteemed parents left." He may have said "esteemed parents," but it didn't sound too respectful. "Your esteemed parents," Votruba went on, "were in high spirits when they left. Unusually high spirits, that's for sure. And your Herr Papa paid from the wallet: one florin seventy-three for the check and fifteen kreutzers tip, ten for me and five for the busboy, I know that for a fact. Here's his beer mat, with nine X's and two O's, nine Pilsners and two small stouts. Your Frau Mama drank those. With the two orders of goulash soup and one herring salad that makes exactly one florin seventy-three. Am I right? Beer prices are going up after the first of January."

The boy took note of the bill and its breakdown. Then he asked again: "What do you think I should do now?"

"The best thing would be to report the loss straightaway to the police. How much was in the wallet?" The boy ignored this question. "Which police?" he asked.

"Maybe at the station on Heinrichsgasse. That's the closest. But you should really go home. It's three-thirty already and we need to close. I live in Smíchov and the others in Koschirsch. We'd be glad to walk you home otherwise. But you live on the opposite end of town. Your father can go to the police tomorrow."

The two underwaiters and the busboy had now put all the chairs on the tables and the taproom looked like it was full of giant beetles lying on their backs with their legs pointing toward the ceiling.

The boy said goodbye and went outside again, heading toward Wenceslas Square. He no longer looked at the sidewalk, for his father couldn't have gone this way. The square was still bustling and the never-ending snowfall did nothing to stop it, indeed even seemed to encourage it. Outside the Golden Goose Hotel a noisy argument had broken out between two rather tipsy groups, one made up of German fraternity students, the other of Czech civilians, each trying through all sorts of heated exclamations and unambiguous taunts to persuade the other of their right to existence. A policeman with a green tuft of cock's feathers tried to put an end to the altercation by repeatedly shouting, "Gentlemen, disperse!" but no one paid him any mind, even though he sometimes appended the words "in the name of the law" to his exhortations. All manner of incendiary slogans were bandied back and forth, "universal suffrage" and "Jungbunzlau District Court" among them. Then suddenly someone stepped up to declare: "The Queen's Court Manuscript proves that Czech culture is older than German." To which the German students protested that the Queen's Court Manuscript was a hoax, but the first speaker emphatically defended himself: "The Germans were still lying around on their bearskins eating acorns when we Czechs were already eating plum pastry." This comment sparked the eagerly awaited free-for-all, with only the policeman's helpless and imploring cries occasionally audible from its midst, which no one heeded anyway.

The boy listened to this uproar for a while — a common enough occurrence in this city, by the way — before walking up Wenceslas Square a bit and turning left onto twilit Heinrichsgasse, at the end of which, across from the massive Heinrich Tower, above a glimmering door of frosted glass, hung an eagle coat of arms with the inscription: "Imperial and Royal Police Station." He hesitated a moment outside the door, for something menacing and disturbing was probably concealed behind it. Then he thought: "I haven't done anything wrong. I'm only here to report a lost wallet and ask for help." Of course, at the same time he dimly perceived his weakened position as a supplicant, and vaguely feared what his father liked to call "the inescapable meshes of the law." Then he remembered the pocketknife. Well, he could mention that, too. Surely he would mention it.

The room was filled with bluish smoke, which acquired an opalescent quality from the yellow-white light of two incandescent gas mantle lamps that imbued the objects and people in the room with a ghostly aura, dissolving their contours and seeming to disembody them. Along the gray walls, a number of smoking policemen and a variety of individuals sat around on armless benches. Through the middle of the room ran an elevated desk, with shelves containing countless bundles of files visible behind it, and above these, hanging in the wispy clouds of smoke, a lifelike oleograph portrait of His Majesty, full-bearded and in field-marshal uniform decorated with the Order of the Golden Fleece. A calm and forbearing Franz Joseph looked down upon his Bohemian subjects. Even the Emperor is here, thought the boy. Below the Emperor and behind the desk sat a gaunt man in an open, bottle-green tunic whose penetrating gaze seemed to be heightened by a pince-nez secured by a little strap. The man's unbuttoned detachable collar lay before him on the desk, next to a cup of coffee, which he constantly stirred with a spoon while he spoke.

"What are you doing here?" one of the policemen asked the boy.

"I want to report something lost."

"Then take a seat and wait for Herr Inspector to call you."

The boy felt a little uneasy, having not mentioned the pocketknife straightaway. The desk, the inspector with the pince-nez, the Emperor's portrait, the purposeful dreariness of the room, the atmosphere of interrogation, sternness and command would have reminded him of a school classroom if it hadn't been for the tobacco smoke, the unbuttoned collar, the coffee cup, the policemen and the other adults, among them three beautiful yet terrifying females who were standing in front of the desk and negotiating with the policeman, who was now stirring his cup of coffee, now taking a sip from it without removing the spoon, even though whenever he drank the weight of the spoon made it slip toward his mouth, which visibly irritated the policeman but not enough for him to remove it.

"I know you three already," he gruffly announced. "I've had each one of you here before. You're a fine trio! You're not on the books."

"I'm an artist," one of the three beauties protested.

"Ah-ha, an artist," the inspector snarled. "I know all about the art you practice. It's lockup for you. The doctor will come tomorrow and then we'll see what gives."

"I won't stand for it," screamed the second woman. "You'll be in for a real surprise when you find out who my uncle is." Her voice cracked and squeaked like a coloratura gone awry.

"I couldn't care less," thundered the inspector, "if your uncle is Count Schnudi or Prince Tschuntscherlini."

"There are laws!" screeched the third prima donna, repeating it multiple times as if she were singing an aria.

"Yes, there are laws!" fumed the inspector, now bringing his fist down on the desk and making his coffee cup jump. "There are laws, and they're made to catch people like you. You're not gonna interpret the law for me." (It sounded as if the mere interpretation of the law was tantamount to an attempt to revoke it.) "Off to jail with you, I say, and that's the end of it. Public nuisance, insulting the honor of an official, vagrancy, resistance to state authority, and who knows what else. On each count two weeks minimum. Take them away!"

The boy was astonished and horrified to see such beautiful and apparently wholly innocent creatures handled so ruthlessly. He expected them to keep defending themselves or that someone would rise to their defense, but the three women began to laugh, lit up cigarettes, and ultimately followed a pair officers through a door at the end of the room, even jesting with them as they did.

"Laws," the inspector started up once again — and he addressed, as it were, an invisible audience over the heads of those present, among whom were a rather scruffy, intoxicated man, a visibly nervous young person with shoddy shoes, and an aloof-looking gentleman who evidently belonged to the "better classes" — "Laws! I'm the law," he said, "I know the legal system. I passed my exams. I'm patient, but I'm nobody's fool. I'm the one wearing the uniform." A number of sentences followed, all starting with the word "I" and replete with power, grandeur, rancor, and deep dissatisfaction. "I've been on duty since six p.m. It's now past four in the morning. And this is my New Year's Eve!"

He heaved a deep sigh. Then he pulled himself together and shouted, "Next!"

The next one was the drunk. "Fellow smashed a streetlight with a rock," explained one of the policemen.

"What's your name?" growled the inspector.

"What difference does it make what my name is?" whined the man. "What difference does it make where I live? I was born, as you can see, Herr Inspector. I was born unlucky. I'm a family man."

"I'm a family man too," shouted the inspector. "We're all family men. But do I engage in disorderly conduct? Do I damage public property?"

"I wasn't in my right mind. It's New Year's, after all. Those are mitigating circumstances. I didn't mean to throw it at the lamp. The lamp just happened to get in the way. They put it up in the wrong place. All the lamps are in the wrong place. Almost everything is in the wrong place."

"Is that so. Well, you're at the right place now. What were you aiming at then?"

"I can't even say for sure anymore. I just felt like throwing a rock. Out of pure enthusiasm. Is a person not allowed to be enthusiastic?"

"You can be as enthusiastic as you like. But you might get punished for it," said the inspector. "Now then, what's your name?"

"Josef Vonasek."

"So, your name is Josef Vonasek. And you've got nothing better to do than smash a streetlight." He turned to the policeman. "Put his head under the pump then lay him down on a plank bed so the fellow can sleep off his enthusiasm. Eight days and a ten-florin fine. But he won't be able to pay it. In that case, fourteen days. Next!"

Vonasek whimpered softly. If the lamp is public property, thought the boy, then it also belongs to Herr Vonasek. At least a small part of it. He himself had often felt the urge to smash a streetlight. The only reason he didn't was because he didn't dare. If he'd had the courage, he would have been punished. But since he was a coward he ended up being rewarded, so to speak. Vonasek was taken away.

Now it was the turn of the nervous young man with the shoddy shoes. The elegant gentleman of the better-off classes rose and stepped forward with him.

"Now then, what have we here?" asked the inspector.

A policeman filled him in: "This lad tried to walk off with this gentleman's coat at Café Maxim, but fortunately we caught him red-handed."

"Your name? Your occupation? But why am I even asking? It's obvious what your occupation is."

"Day laborer."

"Is that so. And the day never comes, am I right? Let me guess: You're the sort that's too light for the heavy work and too heavy for the light kind. Huh?"

"Please," said the nervous young man, "I mistook his coat for mine, that's all. The gentleman's coat looks just like mine. Please take a look and see for yourself. Gray with a herringbone pattern." And he pointed to his shabby coat, one of whose pockets was frayed and torn.

"I was watching him," said the elegant gentleman. "He stood with his coat on his arm at the coatrack, and stayed there for a while. Then he hung up his coat and put on mine. That's when I caught him."

"A waiter attested to it," said the policeman.

"I beg you, Herr Inspector," interjected the young man, "I beg you, it was just an error. To err is human."

"To err is human. But stealing winter coats is not. Animals steal winter coats. Take him away!" The boy wondered what kind of animal might steal a winter coat. Perhaps this person really had mixed up the coats. A waiter, too, couldn't say for sure if it wasn't just an error.

None of the policemen were left in the room. The organs of public security were all in the back rooms busy with the delinquents they'd rounded up. The boy was alone with the inspector. "So, now it's your turn, my boy," said the inspector. "Why aren't you in bed so late at night? And what are you doing here at the police?"

"My father," the boy began.

"What did your father do?" interrupted the inspector.

"My father didn't do anything..."

"That's what they all say. So your father didn't do anything. Did someone maybe do something to *him*?" The inspector seemed to think he was being friendly. Indeed, he was even smiling behind his pince-nez, but his smile was more of a sinister glint.

"No one did anything to my father," said the boy.

"How now? He didn't do anything himself, and no one did anything to him? So why are you here then?"

"My father's wallet..."

"Aha, a wallet," cried the inspector, almost cheerfully. "Now we're getting to the *nervus rerum*." The boy didn't know what these words meant but they sounded awfully menacing. "Before you continue, tell me your father's name, his occupation, his address."

Stuttering, the boy supplied the information requested. "Well then, a civil servant. What happened to the wallet?"

The boy recounted the sequence of events, and his throat ached while doing so. He told about how he searched in the snow on the streets and at the City of Moscow, and explained why his father couldn't look for it himself, on account of his gallbladder.

"Gallbladder? I know about that. He probably overdid it with the fat. Roast goose or something like that. Still, he should have come on his own and not sent you. You can tell him I said that. How much did you say was in the wallet? So much? Well, of course, his New Year's bonus. Tell him we'll cable all the police stations. He should be more cautious if his gallbladder's acting up. He shouldn't eat roast goose. You can tell him I said that too."

"He didn't eat roast goose."

"I didn't ask you what he ate. I'm telling you: he shouldn't eat roast goose. Understood? Everyone eats roast goose and afterwards they all regret it. Sykora!" he shouted then, and after this name was called repeatedly and a policeman appeared from the back rooms he said: "Sykora, take the boy home. He lives . . . well, he'll show you where he lives."

Officer Sykora put on his shako with the greenish shimmering cock's feathers and took the boy by the hand.

"Can't I go home alone?" asked the boy, alarmed. "I haven't done anything wrong." Then he remembered the pocketknife he'd found. But before he could say any more Sykora declared: "Orders are orders. And orders must be obeyed." And with that he pulled him out the door.

"But you don't have to lead me by the hand."

"Fine, you can walk alongside me then," said the policeman, lighting up a stubby pipe.

The feeling of being escorted by a policeman was unpleasant in the extreme to the boy. A fierce defiance reared up inside him. He was twelve years old. Wasn't that worth something? And he didn't need to be escorted down the street and handed over to his parents as if he were some kind of delinquent. He had gone out alone to prove that he was capable of something. He'd wanted to help his father. He loved his father. He loved his father the way he was, including his violent temper and his godlike, face-slapping glory. He wanted to finish this business on his own. He didn't say a word. He racked his brain to find a way to shake off the policeman.

Snow still fell in the murky streets, and only the occasional late pedestrian could still be seen at this hour.

"Well then, yet another new year upon us. You're supposed to make resolutions," observed a jovial Officer Sykora when they reached the edge of the Stadtpark. "Just a moment," he said, and began to relieve himself against a tree. This was the moment the boy had been waiting for, and he seized the opportunity. With a swift leap he cleared a hedge and, running through snow and between the trees, slipped into the dark park.

"Wait, you little rascal! Will you wait!" cried Sykora. "Stop, in the name of the law," and he began chasing after the boy, who, nimbly executing zigzag jumps between the snow-covered bushes and trees, had quickly gained a lead, which grew even bigger when Sykora, after the first few steps, fell flat on his face in the snow then scrambled back to his feet, swearing, and still had to pick up his pipe, having dropped it in the process. But the boy had already escaped, silently he ran through the snow with the speed of a hunted animal, ran as if all the lawmen in town were breathing down his neck. He could still hear from afar the shrill of the police whistle and quickened his pace even more, so that even a much more agile pursuer than the somewhat portly Sykora would have been hard pressed to catch him. Sykora didn't know the boy's address. The inspector had failed to give it to him. That was a good thing. Because he couldn't know where the boy was going.

But while the boy ran he began to feel guilty again. The inspector had entrusted him to the policeman. Sykora, not knowing the address, would have to go back to the station. He would get into trouble, might even be punished for letting his charge get away from him. What's more, the inspector, who was in a foul mood as it was, would draw his conclusions from the boy's escape and obviously assume the worst. After this breach of confidence he would start to doubt everything the boy had said and would possibly think that the wallet incident was nothing but a cock-and-bull story. He would probably never cable the other police stations. Instead, the next day they would summon his father to appear at the station himself — they had his name and address, after all. Besides which, the boy had said nothing about the pocketknife, a search for which was probably underway. Now he had not only jeopardized his chances of getting the wallet back, had not only created unforeseeable problems for Officer Sykora and himself, but had likely implicated his father as well. He had thwarted the designs of officialdom. "Resistance to state authority," is what the police inspector had called it, who ultimately had the best of intentions by instructing Sykora to escort the boy home.

All of these recriminations were drilling into the boy's soul when, having passed Bulgarian Corner, he slowed his pace and made his way through the now completely empty and thickly snow-covered street. He was almost outside the door to his apartment building, house key in hand, when he summoned his strength yet again and resolved to go back to the police station, where — no matter what they might think of him — he would surrender himself to the inspector, confess to his wrongdoing, apologize to him and to Officer Sykora, and furthermore turn in the pocketknife. His throat was killing him. He was sweating, he was parched. But he paid no heed to his body.

Slowly he worked his way back through the snow. He no longer scoured the ground like before. The wallet was not so important anymore. Important was the immensity of his guilt. He broke out in tears from the cold and his grief. His forehead was burning. A feeling of terrible loneliness afflicted him. He failed to understand how a person could feel so afflicted and yet so indescribably lonely.

Just before reaching Bulgarian Corner, he slipped in the snow and stumbled. Balancing on one leg like a dancer, arms stretched wide, the swinging motion of his other foot knocked a dark object out of the snow. He picked it up unthinkingly, utterly indifferent. He could have gone home now and gloried in a grand triumph. But no, he didn't go home. He stuck the find in his pocket and plodded through the swirling snow back to the police station.

Why does a boy walk alone and forlorn through the murky, wintery streets?

I know, because it was me.

PORTER KUBAT

During my adolescence, in the first decade of this century, there still existed in my hometown of Prague the so-called "porters" in red caps. Standing at train-station exits, outside the city's few larger hotels as well as at busy intersections, their job was basically running errands in exchange for a certain fee. They were usually older, slightly weary looking gentlemen whose days in this profession were numbered, as they would soon be replaced by the *Rote Radler,* the young "Red Cyclist" bicycle couriers, who could run any errand much faster. But the porters with their vermillion visor caps and their license numbers in brass were still around for the time being. Some of them had regular customers, their task usually being to deliver flower bouquets or other fragile gifts, sometimes letters or packages, which for one reason or another could not be entrusted to the postal service. These porters had many an important assignment, especially in matters of the heart among the upper classes. Their daily deliveries being limited in number, they set their fees correspondingly high to make it worth their while.

One such porter by the name of Wenzel Kubat had his spot right under the Powder Tower, a Gothic landmark of the many-towered ancient Bohemian metropolis. I have every reason to talk about Herr

Kubat, having once become curiously enmeshed in an important incident in his professional life. He lived in an outlying district of Prague, in the basement of a building I spent some years in myself as a child. The neighborhood had and likely still has its name from the one-eyed Hussite leader Žižka who routed imperial troops during the religious wars of the Middle Ages. Back in my day, the area was populated by low-income civil servants and poor blue-collar workers. Being poor and blue-collar was basically one and the same back then. The people of Žižkov knew, of course, that rich people did their own kind of work, but this work was not for the purpose of sheer survival and therefore, presumably, had a wholly different meaning.

Porter Kubat commanded my respect, first because of his headgear, the only one of its kind in our building, but also because he had a profession that afforded him a glimpse of certain affairs that no one else was privy to and which he occasionally leaked to us. God forbid that he was ever downright indiscreet, he merely used the occasional mysterious hint to underscore his importance. One time he explained to me why he took up the profession of a porter:

"Sitting around on my heinie is not the thing for me. I can't hang around indoors all day like a cobbler or a tailor. Plenty of fresh air, that's what I need. Maybe I should have become a mailman. Too late now, I guess."

Though Czech by birth, Porter Kubat was entirely fluent in German. He came from the Lesser Town of Prague, where the local brand of German — *Kleinseitner Deutsch* — was the second vernacular. It was also referred to as *Sparkassendeutsch,* "savings-and-loan German," on account of its being used by most of the employees of the Bohemian Savings and Loan Association. This German was peculiar for its very pronounced sibilants and a total disregard for umlauts, turning *Frühstück* into *Frischtick,* or *Knödelsuppe* into *Knederlsuppe.* It was a supranational variety of German, and hence symbolic for the multinational character of the Austro-Hungarian Empire.

Tuesdays and Thursdays were Herr Kubat's busiest days. That's when he had "barracks duty," as he liked to call it. On these days he would head early in the morning to the infantry barracks in Karolinenthal, another Prague suburb. He would always spruce himself up beforehand, polish his shoes, attach a shirt-front to his undershirt, and clip onto his rubber collar a "nailed," or ready-made, black bow tie.

"I have to pay another visit to First Lieutenant Zapfner today," he noted with an air of importance. "He always says to me, 'You gonna be my messenger, you gotta look smart.'"

I was eager to know why the errands of First Lieutenant Zapfner required such formal elegance and soon found out that on the days in question Herr Kubat usually had several letters, along with flower bouquets or packages, to deliver to various female addressees.

"Society ladies, all of them," he said.

"So many?" I asked, in disbelief. "And always the same ones?"

"Usually," he said while polishing his brass number plate.

Conversations of this sort between me and Herr Kubat either took place in the morning on my way to school, when I'd pop in at his place for a minute, or in the evening, when I'd run into him while fetching a pitcher of beer for my father from the tavern around the corner. Sometimes, on summer evenings or Sundays, he would sit on an apple crate outside his building. He hardly felt like staying at home in his dismal apartment with his wife, Frau Kubat, a sturdy woman in her fifties, who earned a bit on the side as a housekeeper. She would come to our place two or three times a month, and I'd try to pick up a thing or two from her conversations with my stepmother, or "Step," as I called her for short.

"He's got a second client at the barracks now," I once heard her say, "First Lieutenant Rimoldi, a South Tyrolean with a coal-black mustache. This one also sends letters and little parcels. And what do you know, one of those dames is the same one First Lieutenant Zapfner is corresponding with."

"A fine one she must be," said Step. I was cognizant at an early age that words sometimes meant the opposite of their actual meaning. A "dame" and a "fine one" was not a fine one at all, just like a "gentleman" was rarely gentle.

"And guess what her name is," Frau Kubat went on, "I mean her first name? Melitta, that's what. Ever heard of a thing like that? A decent broad is called Marie or Anna. Must be some kind of foreigner."

"I'm sure she is," announced Step contemptuously.

The expression "some kind of," by the way, was reserved for the lowest of the low on the female social ladder.

It was impossible, of course, to find out any particulars about the contents of the letters written by First Lieutenants Zapfner and Rimoldi. But I soon had an unexpected opportunity to learn what was behind this delicate correspondence. One Thursday, Porter Kubat was given an extra assignment by our landlord that needed to be handled posthaste, for the landlord, Vejvoda, was a fearsome man and you didn't want to get on his bad side.

"Would you like to do me a favor?" Porter Kubat asked me.

"Of course," I said, "gladly."

"I have to run an errand for Vejvoda and can't deliver Zapfner's letter. You wanna do it for me?"

"I've got gymnastics at four on Mariengasse. I could do it."

"Mariengasse? Perfect. The address is: Fräulein Melitta Kisfaludi, corner of Bredauer Gasse and Mariengasse, No. 48, through the courtyard, second staircase, third floor. Just don't lose the letter, for heaven's sake, and don't tell a soul about it."

The building had one of those old Prague courtyards with railed balconies running the length of each floor. I found the door of the apartment easily, what with the "Kisfaludi" calling card tacked to it. I knocked several times and was just about to slip the letter under the door when a young woman opened. She had thrown on a flowered dressing gown, wide open in the front and whose telltale batiste hinted at things that made me lower my gaze.

Fräulein Kisfaludi, whose identity seemed pretty obvious to me, took the letter as if she'd been expecting it and said, "One moment. I might give you a reply."

She let me into the hallway and, remarking that she'd be right back, stole into an adjoining room in her gold-embossed slippers, shutting the door behind her.

Her "right back" took a pretty long time. Maybe First Lieutenant Zapfner's letter was long and meaty, or maybe she needed to think long and hard about what to say in reply. It gave me time at any rate to look around a little. A wardrobe stood in the hallway with a number of suitcases and cardboard boxes piled on top of it. On the wall hung a picture of a horse-drawn sleigh racing through a snow-covered steppe, presumably Russian, which was under attack by a raging pack of wolves. On another wall hung a mirror, with colorful postcards and what seemed to be a couple of bills stuck into its golden frame. In the corner stood her very own dressmaker's dummy, around its neck a nearly fresh laurel wreath complete with a red silk ribbon, on which I could make out the words "Éljen Melitta!" emblazoned in golden letters. I inferred from this that Fräulein Kisfaludi was of Hungarian extraction and had not long ago been the cause of great celebration. I knew the word éljen meant "long live," the triumphant cheer of Magyar magnates used in conjunction with Emperor Franz Joseph.

Fräulein Kisfaludi reappeared after what seemed like ages, still with her gaping dressing gown, but some transformation must have taken place in her, for she now wore a black beauty spot on her cheek that I hadn't noticed before. She handed me a letter, addressed to

First Lieutenant Zapfner in the barracks of Karolinenthal. "Deliver it in person," she said, handing me one crown. I was already out the door when she called me back and gave me a slice of poppy-seed strudel.

In the stairwell I studied the envelope. It was violet with the address written in unusually large and irregular letters — a marked contrast to the first lieutenant's small, calligraphic handwriting, I noticed. I wolfed down the poppy-seed strudel and decided to skip my gym class, which anyway was just an elective. Having agreed to assist Herr Kubat, I couldn't justifiably abandon my mission only halfway through.

And so I rushed to Karolinenthal. At the barracks gate I asked the guard with all the gravity I could muster where I could find Herr First Lieutenant Zapfner, whom I had to deliver a letter to *in person*. I was shown to a special wing of the rather ample building. I walked down barren corridors and looked through the windows at the barracks yard outside, where individual units were performing a number of drills. Finally I found First Lieutenant Zapfner.

"What's the matter with Kubat?" he asked. I explained the situation to him.

"Very well. Here's a crown for you. And tell Kubat to be here the day after tomorrow."

Two crowns, that was a whole florin! I should have actually claimed it as my rightful messenger's fee, for I hadn't just run the necessary errands but even skipped my gym class, which, moreover, I'd have to hide from my father. On the other hand, I felt so richly rewarded by the poppy-seed strudel, the sight of Fräulein Kisfaludi, and having caught a glimpse of the inside of the barracks that when I got home in the evening I handed over to Herr Kubat the whole two crowns and even refused the twenty-five kreutzers he generously offered me in return.

"Don't be stupid," he said, "twenty-five kreutzers are more useful than a florin." You're a good messenger, though. You might amount to something yet."

"Who is Fräulein Kisfaludi, anyway" I asked.

"She's from the theater," he answered, "a lady in the corps de ballet, as they say. One of them dancers. She's even on the playbill."

The playbill was printed each day in the paper. And on one of the following days I saw a note in the program: "Dances, performed by Lina Carmasini, Mizzi Monteverdi, Melitta Kisfaludi, and the ladies of the Corps de Ballet." These names had the ring of magical faraway lands. I later learned, of course, that names could be made to order, when once on the program of a guest performance by Italian opera singers performing in their native language I saw two local artists' names that had obviously been Italianized: "Due Briganti: Philippo Veith, Riccardo Taussig." But Fräulein Kisfaludi seemed like the real deal, the rightful bearer of her name, she being exactly what you imagined a Hungarian woman to be: raven-haired, blazing eyes, bold in profile and proud of bearing.

My father was not a theatergoer. He had no particular dislike of the theater, but a gallery seat cost sixty kreutzers, plus the five additional kreutzers he had to pay to the janitor to let him in at night. A railroad official could rarely afford a thing like that. I myself had only been to the theater for a couple of popular performances at reduced prices, when *The Barometer-Maker on the Magic Island* and *The Fairy Doll* were playing.

But one day Herr Kubat knocked on our door and said to my father: "Would Herr Auditor perchance like to go to the theater today? I've got two free tickets, and it's not my cup of tea anyway." So Father and I went to the theater that evening, a double bill no less, *Cavalleria rusticana* and *Pagliacci*. Step outright declared that she had no interest in joining us, since she couldn't stand the noise. As a safeguard she packed us two anchovy sandwiches and two pieces of crumb cake to take along as a snack.

The theater with its rings of loges, its gigantic chandeliers, the abundance of golden ornamentation, the amoretti that hovered over the box seats and held out little mirrors to each other, the curtain with its procession of all the muses, the obscene amount of red plush, and the many people — all of this was an awesome experience. The cacophony of musical instruments being tuned seemed in its utter confusion to resemble a modern symphony, though perhaps a little more imaginative. But for me the biggest surprise was the playbill, which above the cast announced in red overprint:

Debut!
Owing to the indisposition of Fräulein Stöckler:
SANTUZZA . . . MELITTA KISFALUDI.

"Father, what's an indisposition?" I asked.

"You wouldn't understand . . . It means she suddenly got sick."

"And what does 'debut' mean?"

"Debut? A debut is what they call it when someone performs for the very first time."

"But she's not performing for the first time."

"Who's not performing for the first time?"

"Fräulein Kisfaludi."

"What do you know about Fräulein Kisfaludi?"

"I . . . I saw her name a few times in the paper. On the playbill. Listed with the dancers."

"The rubbish you read! Well, she probably sings, too, and knows the role. Or maybe it's some kind of protection. The other girl's probably sick, so this Kisfaludi is taking her place, her understudy so to speak. Be quiet now, they're about to start."

To the strains of Easter morning soon arose the tragedy of unrequited love, of betrayal and jealousy. Santuzza, as she walked on stage, was greeted with thunderous applause, and I joined in immediately without understanding why we were actually clapping before we even knew how the whole thing would end. The ruffian Turridu filled me with loathing and Lola, the village coquette, was deeply repulsive to me. Santuzza, on the other hand, seemed adorable, devotedly eating her heart out. Stunningly dressed in Sicilian costume, she sang like an angel and I applauded her like mad at the end.

"Stop clapping, you moron, no one's clapping anymore," said my father, unpacking an anchovy sandwich. He let me go to the lobby during the big intermission. "Just don't get lost, make sure you find your way back," he said. He himself preferred to stay put in his seat. In the bustling lobby, where the elegant world promenaded or stood around, I soon discovered an acquaintance. It was First Lieutenant Zapfner, strutting around in a snug dress uniform and patent-leather ankle boots. He set his eye on me, quite literally, for he happened to be wearing a monocle and seemed to be viewing the world through that single eye.

"You're just the man I wanted to see," he said, "hold on one sec!"

With that he removed a calling card from its case, wrote something down on the back with a mechanical pencil — I really envied him that pencil — and, slipping a crown in my hand, said:

"Go down to the stage door, fast, have them take you to Fräulein Kisfaludi, and give her this card. You have to exit onto the street and go around the back, where the Grotto tavern is. The stage door's right across from it."

I didn't need to be told twice, and raced straight down the stairs. I have to admit I was indiscreet and read the card as I ran. It didn't say much. On the front was the name "Karl Zapfner" in copperplate letters and on the back, in the miniscule calligraphic script already familiar to me, the cryptic words: "Eleven o'clock! Csikós must be merry!"

At the stage door I asked for Fräulein Kisfaludi. "What do you want her for?" the doorman barked at me.

"I have to give her something."

"Give it to me then."

"No. I can only give it to her in person. I'm an acquaintance of hers."

"Well, in that case, go left here down the little hallway. Then through the iron door on the right. Someone there will point her out."

Extremely nervous, I opened the heavy iron door and was soon in the labyrinthine world backstage with its scenery, soffits, ropes, cables, set pieces, stagehands, choristers, and all the whirling chaos suffused with dust, rosin and other smells of a theater in the midst of transformation. I asked around, fearful that I wouldn't be able to find her and return to my gallery seat in time. Finally I was shoved through a door and into a changing room where Fräulein Kisfaludi in person was sitting on a pouffe before a mirror, in a slightly grubby gown from which her naked rosy legs protruded.

"What's the matter?" she said when she saw me. "What are you doing here?"

I saw that she recognized me, which made me happy. I handed her the card. She read it, laughed, and tore it to pieces.

"Well?" she said. "Anything else?"

"No," I answered, but couldn't take my eyes off her, couldn't tear myself away from the scent of the little room, the alluring welter of colorful skirts, corsets, stockings, makeup, flacons and flower bouquets scattered all over. She smiled and pinched my cheek.

"Now get out of here, will you!"

I felt the need to express my admiration for her but couldn't find any words. Finally it occurred to me to say something special.

"Éljen Melitta," I cried and ran from the changing room into the street, back up the stairs to the gallery and, completely out of breath, made it to my seat in the nick of time, just as the lights of the auditorium were dimming.

"Why are you panting?" asked Father, but the first chords of *Pagliacci* saved me the trouble of answering.

Fetching the *Tagblatt* from the doorstep the following morning, I immediately read a review of the performance which unfortunately said no more than "Fräulein Kisfaludi commendably handled a difficult task in the part of Santuzza." That was precious little.

"What does the word *csikós* mean?" I asked my father at breakfast.

"Csikós? What do you need to know that for? Csikós are horse herdsmen on the Puszta. Ah, yes, the csikós! There's a song that goes:

> Drink Tokay, it gives you fire!
> Csikós must be merry!

These explanations sufficed, even though it was not fully clear to me what Infantry First Lieutenant Zapfner had in common with a Hungarian horse-herder. Then again, life is varied and people appear in different guises.

I told nothing to Herr Kubat about my dramatic mission during the interlude between the two operas. I even concealed from him the fact that Fräulein Kisfaludi had had a surprise debut as a singer. He probably never learned about it, since he only read a Czech newspaper that deliberately ignored the German theater.

It goes without saying that the recent events I'd blundered into left their mark on me at school. In geography class my mind was more on Melitta in her peignoir than the Northern Limestone Alps; in Latin I dreamt about csikós and could not remember that words that end in -*do*, -*go* and -*io* are feminine; then, in math, I botched a simple equation with a single variable, because the glorious tohubohu backstage was still going through my head. The hours crept by. This day, too, would not be without its sensation.

In the evening I fetched my father's usual liter of beer from the tavern. Supper, I remember precisely, was mutton pilaf with rice. Then everyone minded their own business in the glow of the kerosene lamp. Step knitted wristlets, even though the winter had passed. I rearranged my stamp collection. Father drew the evening paper from his coat pocket, settled down in the rocking chair and began to read. All was quiet, a fairly rare occurrence in my family, the period after supper usually being set aside for domestic quarrels. But my father suddenly broke the silence, casually commenting from behind his paper:

"Well what do you know! That Kisfaludi was found dead this morning."

An earthquake, the sudden eruption of a volcano on our street, a meteor crashing into our living room, or all of this at once would have upset me less than this casual observation, uttered by my father in the same tone he would probably use for relating the current water level.

I asked to see the paper.

"Wait till I've finished reading it."

It took forever. The chief provincial marshal of Bohemia, Prince Lobkowitz, had gone on vacation. The Pilsen brewery increased the price of a pint of beer by a kreutzer. ("Outrageous! Before you know it we'll have no choice but to stop drinking beer altogether!") Admiral Robert Peary reached the North Pole with a Negro and four Eskimos. ("Those Americans!") The "Crown Princess" blouse store changed owners. Joke corner. "What? You put a photo of your wife on your cigarette case? You must really love her." — "Love her? I'm trying to quit smoking."

It nearly drove me to distraction. Finally I got my hands on the paper.

The dancer and singer Melitta Kisfaludi, who just yesterday made her successful debut, was found dead in her apartment this morning. No statement has been issued about the cause of her death, but evidence suggests that the artiste met a tragic end. An autopsy has been ordered. The body was found by a porter delivering a letter to her. Interrogated by the police, he said he had knocked on her door a number of times. When no one answered, he tried to slip the letter under the door. In doing so, the unlocked door opened. The porter found the deceased on the sofa and immediately notified the police, who are still investigating the matter. More in our morning edition!

My first inclination was to run straight down to Herr Kubat. But a choking fear stopped me. Suddenly I'd been implicated in a tragedy, perhaps I myself had been an unwitting instrument in the events that transpired in Melitta's apartment after her momentous opera debut.

"What's the matter? You're all bent out of shape," said my father.

"But I just saw her yesterday evening."

"Who? Oh, you mean that Kisfaludi. So it is: Proudly rode they yester morn, who today by bullets torn," he concluded.

It was clear that the porter in question was none other than Herr Kubat. In the days that followed he became a public figure. I tried my best to avoid him. But in our building, on our street, everywhere in town, people were talking about the young diva's mysterious demise. Every morning, before bringing the early edition to Father, I anxiously read the latest report on the Kisfaludi affair:

All evidence indicates that the artiste had received a visitor before her death. The letter that the porter Wenzel Kubat was unable to deliver was from an acquaintance and contained a congratulatory note on her success as well as an invitation to a rendezvous. The postmortem examination has revealed that the shot to the heart that felled Fräulein Kisfaludi was fired at close range. The weapon, a small-caliber pearl-handled revolver, lay under the sofa near the right hand of the deceased, who was subsequently identified as its owner. The investigation is ongoing.

I ran into Herr Kubat on the day this report was published. He looked at me severely and said, "Haven't seen you for a few days now."

Trying not to seem too self-conscious, I asked how he was doing.

"Not so hot. They're talking and writing about me, alright. But I'm not getting any more work. Neither from Zapfner nor from Rimoldi. A calamity like this makes customers skittish."

"Herr Kubat," I said, "can I ask you something?"

"Everyone's picking my brains these days. What do you wanna know?"

"Who wrote the last letter to the Fräulein?"

"Well, that's no secret. It's even in the police reports. It was from Rimoldi. He had barracks inspection at night and wrote to her in the morning."

"And First Lieutenant Zapfner?"

"He heard her sing at the theater then went to the barracks and hit the sack. It just occurred to me, you must have heard her that evening too."

"Yes, I also heard her sing."

We were silent for a while.

"Herr Kubat, what did the Fräulein . . . how did she look when you found her?"

"Lovely, that's how. You paid her a visit once too. But you'd better keep your mouth shut or you'll run into trouble and so will I. She looked like she was sleeping. 'Madam,' I says, 'here's a letter from Herr Rimoldi.' But she just lies there and doesn't answer. 'Maybe you had a little too much Tokay?' I ask, because I saw a bottle right there. Again no answer. I took her by the hand, and that's when I noticed what a mess I was in. Yep, she was a beauty alright, and a good, honest woman. Always gave me nice tips. Really a shame what happened to her."

Frau Kubat discussed the case in more detail with my step.

"Her relatives from Kecskemét came to the funeral," said Frau Kubat. "My husband was there too. He even took a carriage. The whole theater showed up. And Herr Podlesny, the doorman from the theater, told my husband: 'Herr Kubat, you may as well go to the funeral so it's not a total loss.' Afterwards they drank black beer at the Flora."

"Those broads from the theater, they'll do it with anyone," moralized my step. "Small wonder it ends like this."

"Right you are," said Frau Kubat. "Back in the days when we had a real apartment, we once had a roomer, he was also from the theater. I asked him one Sunday while straightening up: 'Don't you ever go to church?' I was trying to put an idea in his head since I wanted him out for a while. 'To church?' he said. 'No. Or sometimes just for fun.' That's the theater type for you."

"I always say," explained my step, "that nothing good comes of those theater types. You have to keep your distance from them. A woman like that is capable of anything. Whaddaya cookin' today anyway?"

"I'm making apple baba. I've got some old bread rolls to soak, and Kubat loves it 'cause he's almost got no teeth left."

They talked as if Fräulein Kisfaludi hadn't died herself but had murdered someone else.

I wandered a lot around town those days. My conscience was

troubling me. Maybe I should have come forward and told them about the message First Lieutenant Zapfner had had me deliver to Melitta. It was one of many things that were weighing heavily upon my soul. There seemed no end of them.

In my desk drawer, for example, was an iron cannonball the size of a fist, dating from the Hussite Wars. It had once been cemented in a wall on Žižka Hill as a kind of memorial, before I'd chiseled it out with my pocketknife and taken it home with me. It was public property, so I didn't dare go back. On steep Orebitská Street one evening I gave a push to a handcart parked there and sent it hurtling down the street. Who knows what havoc it wreaked. Maybe the cart ran somebody over. As for me, I ran away. In the Stadtpark by Franz Joseph Station, I once tossed a dead sparrow to a stork. I could still see it clearly, how the fat morsel made a bulge in the stork's neck and wandered down its gullet. I never saw the stork again after that. Perhaps I was guilty and had caused its death. I had a lot to answer for. Not paying the bridge toll and riding the tram without a ticket were the least of it. There was no telling how many ways I might have been at fault.

I was plagued by fear at every conceivable moment: when the paper came in the early morning, on my way to school, during class, at home, when falling asleep and even in my dreams, when a policeman so much as looked at me, when a letter came, when a teacher stopped me in the hallway. Now my goose is cooked! They'll start asking questions! Why didn't you tell the police? Who else is involved? Father found me looking pale. He bought me iron-somatose. But my paleness didn't go away. I tossed down a sewer grate the crown that First Lieutenant Zapfner had given me as a messenger's fee that evening at the opera. But maybe someone saw me do it. Who would throw away money? What could be more suspicious than that?

To top it all came Easter, with Confession and Communion. We students went to the Emmaus Monastery for confession, and I made up my mind to come clean. But my courage failed me inside the confessional. I confessed to everything except what really counted.

"Say three Our Fathers and three Hail Marys."

I did my penance of prayer, fasted in the morning, but I knew I'd received the Eucharist in a state of sin. They called that *Gottesraub* — robbing the Almighty. I was now in conflict not only with the world but with God Himself into the bargain. Yet God, preoccupied with the greater cares of the universe, paid no attention to me, or perhaps he did pay attention but figured he had enough time to spare, what with eternity being His. Melitta stood in this eternity and pointed down at me. Her hand would never tire. And God would never tire. No iron-somatose would help against it, even though the dust eventually settled and the tragedy, to all appearances, had been relegated to the files.

One afternoon — it was summer already — Porter Kubat told me, "Zapfner and Rimoldi each gave me two letters to deliver. All of them to officers. Four letters, all for delivery today to completely different districts. Maybe you could take care of one."

"I'd prefer not to," I said.

"You're on vacation. There's nothing to it. You can keep the whole tip."

"It's not about the tip . . ."

"What then? All you do is drop off the letter and finito, you're done! Here, there's one from Zapfner. To Cavalry Captain Habada, Brückengasse 15, in the Lesser Town. You can do that for me, can't you?"

Yes, I could do it. I had done all kinds of things already so I might as well do that, too. I was always a mixture of strength and weakness, tenacity and acquiescence, courage and cowardice. Who knows what might happen if I deliver another letter! But I just couldn't bring myself to say no to Herr Kubat. Anyway, I wouldn't be guilty regardless of what happened. If that were the case, every single mailman would break down under the weight of his guilt! But if you think about it, shouldn't he? Shouldn't that happen to anyone who makes himself an instrument of documents unaware of their implications? For wasn't it written: "It must needs be that offenses come; but woe to that man by whom the offense cometh!"?

All the same, I took the letter and set off into town, past the Powder Tower and Old Town Hall with its astronomical clock, through the warren of narrow streets to Charles Bridge with its stone figures. "The bridge is reach'd, now, Fritz, how wilt thou speed?" The sun was encroaching from beyond the cathedral, groping for the glo
rioles of the saints on the bridge and the ring of stars of my namesake, about whom it was said that his keeping the Seal of Confession had earned him his martyr's crown. Some were skeptical about this story, but the martyr's crown was certain either way. The righteous of the triumphant Church loomed enormously down a long avenue on either side of the bridge, warningly looking down at me from their concave pupils.

Captain Habada looked the way you'd imagine an active-duty cavalry captain. Tall, lean and elegant, he sat with his legs crossed nonchalantly at a little oriental hammered-brass table, smoking a cork-tipped cigarette. I saw him obliquely through the open door from where I was standing in the anteroom, while at the behest of the orderly, or "pipe lid" as they called it in the Austro-Hungarian army, I waited for an answer. Captain Habada read the letter then laid it down on the table before him, seemingly lost in contemplation. This contemplation took quite a while, and was accompanied by the oscillating movements of his right foot. Then he got up and began to pace the room. Now and then he mumbled to himself. The pipe lid meanwhile sat across from me in the anteroom, reading a newspaper. After a while Captain Habada picked up the letter again, read it one more time, and lapsed anew into contemplation.

It was very stuffy in there. A big fat fly buzzed in through the open window of the anteroom, set its sights on the captain's room and, spiraling several times in midair, landed on the letter. It wandered around a bit, traversed the edges of the sheet of paper, probed its lines, then abruptly flew back out the window the same way it had come in. I wondered why this fly, apparently coming from afar, had sought out this very sheet of paper and where it was taking its newfound knowledge.

At last Captain Habada called into the anteroom: "No reply!"

The orderly lowered his newspaper and, as if he assumed the captain's words could only reach him and never me, repeated, "No reply!"

I got up and left.

"When it rains, it pours," Herr Kubat said to me a few days later.

"What happened this time?" I asked.

"Now I've lost Zapfner for good, and Rimoldi into the bargain."

"How come?"

"Zapfner's dead, or rather . . . Well, some things it's better not to talk about. And Rimoldi's been transferred."

"What happened to First Lieutenant Zapfner?"

"I already told you, he's dead. And they sent Rimoldi to Galicia."

"Was Zapfner ill, or what?"

"He who asks much learns much, but he who asks too much learns nothing. He's dead and that's that, *basta fidli!*"

Once Herr Kubat had uttered the words "*basta fidli*" there was no getting anything out of him then. *Basta fidli* meant end of discussion, period. *Basta fidli* was like God concluding Creation: it was pointless to want to add anything, to expect any more from Him.

I began to make the connection when the next day I heard my step and Frau Kubat analyzing the latest news.

"What do you say to that, Frau Auditor! Such a dashing young man!"

"Did you know him, Frau Kubat?"

"Not really, just from hearsay. But it goes without saying he was young and handsome. Else he wouldn't have been a first lieutenant."

"I'm telling you, the girl is behind it all. A woman like that brings bad luck even from the grave. Where did it happen?"

"At five in the morning out at Malvazinky. It's actually forbidden, but officers still do it all the same."

"Yup, they've got what you might call a sense of honor. But they're stupid anyway. A hussy like that isn't worth the trouble."

"If she'd been a decent girl at least! Our sort cooks and launders and darns, and no one gives a hoot about us."

I thought to myself: If I hadn't delivered the letter to Captain Habada, things might have taken a different turn. More time would have elapsed, and more time means more deliberation, it means all sorts of additional factors, new events intervening. A few hours more and the whole world has transformed; what seemed important is suddenly trivial, hot turns cold, fury turns into kindness. Why did I have to deliver that letter! I'd sensed that something wasn't right. I'd balked from the very start. The saints on the bridge were warning me. Each time I passed one I could have turned back. I fell into a heap and sobbed: "God, give every person time!"

Or was it maybe the right thing after all for me to deliver the letter? Was it not me, and precisely me, who formed the necessary link in a chain, an inevitable development leading to a higher good? Drink Tokay, it gives you fire! It made no difference and prevented nothing, my keeping silent about Zapfner's message to Melitta. Fate achieves its aim in a roundabout way if necessary. But what wrong did Zapfner actually do? Only one man might have known, and he'd been transferred to Galicia. But maybe even he didn't know what really transpired in that apartment behind the old courtyard gallery, and the tragic aftermath of the whole tragic affair was fueled by suspicions and speculation.

The strange thing was how, in the wake of this final incident, an inexplicable sense of calm ultimately overcame me. And this, more than any train of logic, seemed to confirm that a mysterious equilibrium had been attained, and that the role that I'd been delegated must have had its justification and served a meaningful purpose. Such calm does not emerge if the cosmic lines of force are disturbed. I gradually stopped enumerating all of my many transgressions. I brazenly placed on my desk the Hussite cannonball; the dead stork and the free-rolling handcart no longer troubled me. No hand in eternity was pointing down at me anymore. I could stop taking iron-somatose. Éljen Melitta!

Not long afterwards we moved to a different neighborhood. And not long after that an entire decade passed. Even then I sometimes saw Porter Kubat standing at his usual spot below the Powder Tower. He seemed no older than before. The towers of Prague didn't seem any older either, nor did the saints on the bridge or the astronomical clock on the Town Hall. He stood there with his red cap and shiny brass number plate, on the lookout for clients.

"There's less and less of 'em," he told me the last time I saw him. "Those were the days, back when you used to help me out. Now everyone's using those newfangled bicycle messengers. The personal touch, no one appreciates that these days."

"Herr Kubat," I said, somewhat abashed, "I've got a little job for you. This letter. It's very important to me . . ."

"What? A delivery?" he said, overjoyed. He took the letter and studied the address. "Well look at that! To a lady from the theater! Youth must have its fling. *Basta fidli!*"

WE STOOD HONOR GUARD

I only lived through the last two decades of the Francisco-Josephinian era, and actually only just the last one with an awakening and ever-clearer consciousness. The Emperor himself I saw just once in Prague. I was a Gymnasium student when His Majesty in his equipage rode down the Franzensquai promenade up to Castle Hill, his governor, Prince Thun, at his side, "long Franzel" as they used to call him. We German high schoolers cheered him on. The Czechs beside us remained icily, hostilely silent. The equipage rolled past us slowly, and we saw the Emperor for about a minute. He waved mechanically to Germans and Czechs alike, and the light-green tuft of feathers on his shako, which looked like some jolly Christmas-tree ornament, waved along with him above his ruddy face framed by a white round beard. The year was 1908. The Prince of Peace had just annexed Bosnia and Hercegovina. A song that the Czechs sang in every Prague tavern provided a political commentary on this event:

> For the emperor, our lord,
> and his family
> we had to free
> Hercegovina.

I went to elementary school in a Prague suburb. Classes were conducted in German, but the pupils were mostly Czech proletarian children on account of the free lunch sausage for those of lesser means. This sausage notwithstanding, these children never tired of mocking Austria, Vienna, the Germans, the Habsburgs and the Emperor, whom they called *"Procházka,"* a nickname that, in itself, was hardly cause for ridicule — the word means "walk" or "stroll," an activity that certainly has nothing objectionable about it — especially considering that many Czechs and indeed Bohemian Germans used it as a surname, even those of noble birth. It wasn't the word itself but the way it was used that lent it its offensive character. A judge, for instance, once convicted a Prague market woman for impugning the honor of a neighboring market woman by calling her a "symphony." During the Emperor's visit, a hawker at a major Prague intersection was crying his wares with the slogan *"hole na procházku,"* and its derisive double meaning in Czech — "walking canes for caning Procházka" — was soon heard all over town. I don't think anyone put the man up to it. He did it of his own accord, following his own spontaneous creative inspiration, which happened to reflect the mood of thousands of Czechs.

Why did the Czechs despise and deride Emperor Franz Joseph so much? The political answer usually went: because he hadn't had himself crowned King of Bohemia in Prague and — succumbing to Hungarian pressure — held fast to Austro-Hungarian dualism instead of transforming it into an Austro-Slavic-Hungarian trialism. But this answer, like all political answers, was merely an excuse. I think that my Czech classmates and countrymen hated the Emperor and the Habsburgs from the depths of their souls and with the same kind of hatred that is otherwise reserved for Jews, or in some parts of the world for colored people. The reasons offered are always rational, but the truth is people just want to hate. Of course the Czechs were not alone in feeling hatred; other nations did as well. Coming to Vienna from northern Germany, Christian Friedrich Hebbel railed against the Czechs, disparaging them, quite irrationally, as a "servant people." The imperial government should have taken this uncouth foreigner, applauded by a foolish intellectual clique, and driven him out of the country for slandering one of its peoples. It didn't, for it was liberal in tolerating insults aimed at those in the opposition. There was the rub, as always and everywhere.

The establishment of universal suffrage did nothing to lessen the hatred Czechs felt. It had been around for too long. There was no statute of limitations on this hatred, it had been around since the Battle of White Mountain; since the execution of the Bohemian noblemen on Old Town Square; since the erection of the Marian column in front of Old Town Hall, not for inspiring piety but as a symbol of political humiliation. This hatred did not go away when they toppled the Marian column in 1918 and Habsburg rule came to an end. Hatred bred hatred. And when such a hatred grows old it does not become infirm with age; it propagates, regenerates itself, continues to feed off itself even when its immediate causes have seemingly long since vanished. "I hate, therefore I am," is one of the most passionate criteria of existence among nations.

The question of why the Francisco-Josephinian era (including the brief reign of Charles) actually came to an end repeatedly elicits all manner of possible historical, political and other explanations, enough to fill up thick books and which, taken on their own, may ring true, but that nevertheless mean very little. For they are only symptoms of an overall attitude. And this overall attitude in the Austro-Hungarian Empire was characterized by utter lovelessness, by the absolute lack of kindness or the willingness to ever do anything for anyone except oneself, by the indescribable callousness and selfishness of everyone. It was the ignominy of an all-embracing mutual lovelessness that ultimately destroyed that era. And if one objects that selfishness is fundamental to being human, is a part of our individual, social and political nature, the answer to this is simple: it's exactly what ruins human beings and empires, what has always ruined them, and what will keep on ruining them in the future, however rich or powerful they might happen to be at times. As Heinrich Mann once so magnificently expounded during the First World War, this was what ruined the Second French Empire, what ruined czarist Russia, Wilhelmine and Hitlerian Germany, Britain's world empire, the list could go on and on, backwards and forwards, as long as it is selfishness that underlies the political rationales ostensibly causing these collapses — ostensibly because empires do not fall apart due to external causes but begin to crumble from within. These may be truisms. But, as Goethe once remarked, we have to keep on repeating the truth, since the falsehoods all around us are constantly being repeated as well.

In the Austro-Hungarian Empire, everyone hated and no one loved. Everyone sought their own advantage, no one was willing to make a sacrifice. At best they made a deal and cheated their way around it. How was such an empire supposed to hold together? I firmly believe that we German poets and writers in Old Prague were the only ones who honestly tried to spread the ideas of love and reconciliation. Rilke did it, Werfel did it, Kafka did it, Brod and all the rest of us. *The Friend of the World*, *The Height of Feeling*, *One Another* and *Feast of Reconciliation* were the titles of German books from Prague, and I edited a journal called *Humankind*. And what did we reap in return, even from the most magniloquent and fiercest critic of our day, who also happened to be our fellow countryman? Scorn and contempt, corny puns and mockery, which was worse than the utter lack of interest we encountered from our Czech neighbors, even though we lovingly translated them. The nobility, by nature dynastic and supranational, hovered too much above it all, bore the Emperor aloft like a cloud, and was incidentally no less self-absorbed than all the others. A common empire would have only been possible by means of loving concessions, and the same goes for a common Europe, and a common world as well.

This is the instructive legacy that the era of Franz Joseph bequeathed to humanity, and which humanity could well use to finally gain an awareness that the ignominy of lovelessness is what makes empires fall.

THE LAST TOMBOLA

The following is a faithful retrospective snapshot of real events, characters and sensibilities.

My father, who always used to say, "It's no good eating cherries with me" — meaning, "I'm not a pleasant person to deal with" — whenever he sent me on one of his errands, had given me orders (because back then everything was an order) to make a detour on my way to school one morning, that is to the Imperial and Royal State Gymnasium with German as the language of instruction, located on the Graben in Prague's second district, where I happened to be in the second form at the time. My task was to deliver a thick envelope to Railroad Inspector Pernold, who was staying at the Imperial Hotel on Na Poříčí, or Porschitsch as it was known in German. Na Poříčí is Czech for "on the riverbank," which is fair enough, since the Moldau flows nearby. Still, I had an instinctive aversion to this Prague street, its two chafing affricates reminding me of the sand-yellow paletot that hugged the hips of my stepmother around the time my father was courting her. I had witnessed this courtship and once heard her say, "It chafes me; I bought it on Na Poříčí." "Good," I remarked, because I felt this lady couldn't be chafed enough. "Who asked you?" asked my father. "I asked me," I answered. He was about to give me a royal smack in the face, which was usually accompanied by the words, "When duty calls, feelings must be silent." Yet this time he abstained from getting violent, not wanting to appear ungallant in front of the lady. He looked at me instead like Cronus before he ate his children.

Whatever the case, I had to make a detour through Na Poříčí. It was quarter to eight in the morning, and I was thirteen years old. I knew Herr Pernold well, and liked him a lot. "Liked him a lot" in this case means I didn't like him a lot but I kind of liked him, which is to say, I thought he was okay, or that I liked him but not everything about him, just some things. One of the things I liked was his truly Viennese love of music, which found expression in the fact that he used to always hum to himself what he described as an old Austrian folk song that went: "Why shouldn't I be merry when grief and pain oppress me?" Herr Pernold was the auditor of the Reichenberg–Gablonz–Tannwald Railroad, whose accounts were kept by my father. This local railroad was the only Bohemian one in private hands but was nonetheless state-run, which is why my father entered its receipts and expenditures in the books of the Imperial and Royal State Railway Administration. All other Bohemian local railroads, whose accounts my father likewise supervised, were long since nationalized and hence passive. The Reichenberg–Gablonz–Tannwald Railroad was active, and brought its shareholders considerable annual dividends, passing as it did through wealthy industrial regions. None of this was new to me, because each Christmas my father would receive from the Vienna administration a bonus, or "remuneration," of one hundred florins for his satisfactory bookkeeping. From this bonus he bought me ice skates — "Halifax" brand, the screw-on kind, and thus inferior to "Jacksons," which were fastened directly to the shoe sole, but at least they were ice skates — the only "fun" present I ever got from him, and this, by the way, secondhand from a junk dealer on Galligasse, half price, because ice skates are ice skates, who needs new ones? The screws didn't screw well and the skates were wobbly before you even got going. Susi Gerstel naturally had factory-made Jacksons that were curved at the end, and she skeptically eyed the pointed ends of my Halifaxes, but poverty, of course, is splendor from within.

So Herr Pernold made an appearance each year, coming all the way from Vienna. He inspected my father's bookkeeping and determined to what extent it deserved remuneration. The word "remuneration" was one of my earliest linguistic and cultural assets. Everything that had to do with Herr Pernold was important, which is why the envelope I was supposed to bring him had to be important too. But Herr Pernold was crucial to my development for yet another reason. He and the spouse he sometimes brought with him, known as Frau Pernold, were the only guests my father ever had over for dinner, the only ones he ever invited at all. Herr Pernold usually came alone. But once or twice he brought his wife (more about her in a moment). We never had company otherwise. When, for instance, my stepmother's sister dared to stop by for coffee and my father unexpectedly entered the room — which always had something menacing about it, like sheet lightning — my step-aunt would get up at once and exit without a word. Not that she and my father were enemies, or that she had something against him, she just had the feeling that she'd done something reprehensible, or at least committed an irregularity, or that perhaps her very existence somehow made her wrong, a fact which seemed to be confirmed through various, mumbled incidental remarks made by my father: "Long hair, short wit," "No front and no behind," or suchlike. But whenever Herr Pernold came to Prague he would always dine with us at least once. Not that my father harbored any feelings of friendship for him. I didn't know anyone at all who might have been called my father's friend. Maybe he even hated him. The dinners weren't proof of anything. I knew, for example, that

Father despised his head clerk, Chief Inspector Slezina, "that ratfink." And yet each time Christmas came around I had to walk to the Smíchov district with my father and deliver an eighteen-pound ham to Slezina's apartment. My father carried the ham to the door of the building and I had to lug it up four floors (the first and second plus the raised ground floor and mezzanine levels, both unnumbered) and ring Slezina's bell. Usually a female with greenish hair would open, presumably Ratfink's wife. I assumed she was splenetic, because *slezina* means "spleen" in Czech. So there was really no way of telling if my father felt any real attachment to Herr Pernold, even though on the evening before my errand he had eaten dinner at our place: roast goose with sauerkraut and Bohemian dumplings, preceded by beef broth with sponge dumplings, and apple strudel for desert, whose thin dough, when raw, was stretched to the size of a double bed sheet. As always, it was my duty to go to the Frog tavern and fetch a two-liter pitcher of Pilsner for this never-changing meal whenever Herr Pernold came to visit. The year before he'd been accompanied by his wife, who was considerably younger than him. His hair was thinning and his teeth going brown while she, with her prominent bosom, went on and on about Marienbad, in particular about some officer there, whom she referred to as her cousin. "Cousin, ha-ha, that's a good one," said my stepmother in the kitchen. "What's good about him?" I asked. To which she replied: "I didn't say *he's* good, I said it's a good one — a likely story." "What does likely mean?" At which point the conversation ended. But that, like I said, was the year before. This time Herr Pernold came alone.

The envelope from my father in the one hand, my book bag — likewise secondhand, from Galligasse — in the other, I entered the vestibule of the Imperial Hotel, which had nothing imperial about it at all, but was dark and stuffy, with scruffy leather furniture. I went to the desk, where a gold-braided porter, a waiter, a chambermaid, a valet in striped overalls, a cleaning woman with a scrub bucket, and two or three other indefinable persons were all talking at the same time in what seemed to be a state of nervous excitement. I would never have made my presence felt if the gold-braided porter hadn't asked me: "What do *you* want?"

His emphasis on the familiar "you" offended me. Why shouldn't I be there? I had legitimate independent affairs to take care of. The nerve of this hotel employee trying to play *frère et cochon* with me, a young man who already had his own calling card with the words "stud. gym." printed on it. I knew the French phrase from a dictionary of foreign words. Besides which, as a second-former I attached great importance to being addressed with due respect, especially by a hotel porter. Incidentally, it was my godfather Joseph, my father's cousin, who had had the calling cards printed for my last name day. "What do you need calling cards for, you blockhead?" my father had asked at the time. "Why can't you ask for something more sensible — underwear, for example, or handkerchiefs?" But I'd insisted on the calling cards with "stud. gym." on them. So I pulled out one of my cards and said, "May I speak to Herr Pernold?"

"No," said the porter, without so much as glancing at the card, "you certainly cannot speak to him."

"But I must speak to him."

"No one can speak to Herr Pernold."

"But I have to, at once, I don't have time to waste, you know."

The porter's face, which took on a bellicose mien under his peaked cap with its military-like decorations, twisted into an Asiatic grin, revealing pointed, wolfish teeth. "You have to speak to him, huh? And why is that?"

"I have a letter for him."

"A letter? Hand it over."

"I have to deliver it personally."

At that they all broke into a ghastly laughter, the porter, the waiter, the valet, the two women, the whole vestibule was filled with their uncanny, sneering laughter in every imaginable tone high and low, from the midst of which I soon made out the voice of the porter, weeping with delight: "Personally, ha-ha-ha, he wants to speak to him personally!" and they all joined in an uproarious chorus, "personally, ha-ha-ha, personally!"

"Why can't I speak to him in person?" I asked, so furiously that the laughter stopped.

"I'll tell you why, young man," explained the porter, "I'll tell you exactly why. You can't give the envelope to Herr Perold personally because Herr Pernold hung himself last night."

"How come?" I managed to stammer, turning these two syllables into six.

The roaring laughter started up again. "How come, he asks!" cried the porter. "I can't tell you how come. But I can tell you how. With his suspenders, that's how. He hanged himself, and now he's dead. The police are in his room as we speak."

The word "police" gave my limbs the spring of an antelope. Two leaps were all it took and I was out of the vestibule and onto the street, where I was promptly swallowed up by the morning rush of people hurrying to work. I knew the first thing I had to do was bring the envelope to my father, to the barracks-like building of the State Railway Administration where he performed his duties. It wasn't far. I ran. Hanged by his suspenders. Herr Pernold's suspenders were something special, as was his clothing in general. He usually wore a suit made of salt-and-pepper tweed, underneath it a green cloth vest with Salzburg silver buttons that lent him the air of a hunter, an impression already suggested by his pike-gray loden inverness cape, and even more so by his mountain-happy hat with a green cord and tuft of chamois hair, or *Gamsbart*. "A Seppl hat," said Pernold, "it's from

Ischl, where the Emperor also goes chamois hunting." Herr Pernold seemed to vaguely imply that he himself, on His Majesty's hunting grounds, had stalked the chamois that gave his hat the traditional tuft. Upon closer inspection, however, I noticed that the hat was manufactured by the Habig company in Vienna. But a *Gamsbart* is a *Gamsbart,* whichever way you take it. You would hardly believe that all of this flashed through my mind while racing through the streets. All of this and then some. The all-important suspenders, too. Herr Pernold wore his green vest open underneath his coat. It offered a view of his pale-green-striped poplin shirt, and over that the horizontal strap of his suspenders with the words *Grüss Gott!* embroidered on it in colored thread. "Time saver," explained Herr Pernold. "Normally you wear them with lederhosen, the lederhosen with knee-socks, the knee-socks with Goiserer shoes. One thing leads to another. But I wear them with everything, because my late mother embroidered them and gave them to me for my high-school graduation. She told me: 'These will last you. Don't ever forget your little old mother.'" And now Pernold had hanged himself with his beloved suspenders. I couldn't fathom why. I had heard of suicides now and then, but never had it occurred to me that I might have something to do with one myself. Now there was one in my midst, and one who yesterday evening at eight o'clock had enjoyed a leisurely meal of roast goose with us. He had left at ten, with the words: "My best compliments." Those were his final words. What was there to compliment? What could have possibly happened between ten in the evening and eight in the morning to bring about such a decision? Just the night before, he'd been singing to the piano accompaniment of my father. "In forest wild I shoot the stag," and so forth until the end, where it goes: "Yet I, a poor boy starry-eyed, still feel the pangs of love." He'd grinned when he sang the word "boy." Understandably. What, by the way, was "yet" supposed to mean? In spite of what or whom — that wasn't clear

— did he still feel the pangs of love? And why? These are things I should have thought about. I knew, of course, that singing songs was not necessarily a sign of cheerfulness. Once, for example, I heard our janitor, Herr Řepa, merrily singing "I once went to the Vršovice kermis . . . ," and after the song's final verse he threw a bowl of tripe at his wife's head, Frau Řepová. I know for sure it was tripe because I witnessed the scene myself, having stopped by to drop something off at their place. People were always using me to drop things off. I was always running through streets and from floor to floor with notes, letters, and messages for other people. That's pretty much my life. And whenever you have to drop something off, awful things always seem to happen. Now I had a thick envelope in my hand with supplements to the annual balance sheet of the Reichenberg–Gablonz–Tannwald Railroad, which my father had worked on late into the night after Herr Pernold's departure. That's what he got the remuneration for. My father was dutiful, even after roast goose. If he had put it off, he couldn't have sent me to Herr Pernold, and I'd have long since been sitting in class taking a math test. I didn't mind missing that at all, and on account of a suicide into the bargain. That was unbeatable. In the midst of these ambulatory, kaleidoscopic considerations, I reached the railway administration at the corner of Bolzanogasse and was now running up stairs and down hallways, past countless numbered, frosted-glass doors to the third-floor office of my father. To me, this building as a locus of human aspirations had always had something fantastic about it. I knew the Austrian civil-service hierarchy from Father's lectures: Aspirant, Assistant, Adjunct, Auditor, Chief Auditor, Inspector, Chief Inspector — I didn't dare go any further. My father was just an auditor, but Herr Slezina, aka Ratfink, or sometimes just plain scoundrel, nevertheless — or maybe for this very reason — had the rank of inspector, which is why for Christmas I'd bring him a Chmel smoked ham, wrapped first in tin foil, then in green tissue paper, and tied together with red twine. The goods of this world are unevenly distributed.

My father sat hunched over a giant cashbook and was adding up an enormous column of figures. "Behind him, on a colored map, proudly stretched Old Austria." My friend Werfel wrote those lines years later, but it was true back then. My father held the thumb of his left hand under the number he was adding and with the thumb of his right hand tapped the keys of the adding machine — a gadget he'd invented himself, a metal instrument with a numeric keypad, triple patented: in Austria, Hungary, and Germany. This was practically the only existing prototype. "In your head," my father used to say, "you can add much faster, actually, except that it's usually wrong, while with the machine you're slower but you don't make mistakes. Take your pick." He raised his head when I entered but left his fingers right where they were, probably fearing he'd lose his place and have to start all over again adding the long column. He eyed me, concerned and suspicious, and saw the envelope in my hand.

"What do you think you're doing here? Why didn't you drop off the envelope? How come you're not at school?"

Fathers are always asking several things at once. I only had a single answer: "Herr Pernold hung himself."

"What?" shouted Cronus, leaping from his chair in spite of the sum of numbers, which had now been lost for good, and giving me a resounding slap in the face, the force of which sent me flying against the green-bound volumes containing the full Regulations for Transportation on State Railways of the Kingdoms and Lands Represented in the Imperial Council, no less.

"What do you mean, hung?" he then roared, as if this word weren't explanation enough.

"Hanged on his *Grüss Gott* suspenders," I said, handing him the envelope. My cheek still smarted but I was far from taking his outburst amiss. I'd expected something like this. And we had our better hours, as allies in the struggle against my stepmother. This time I was even delighted to take a slap in the face, because I knew he'd committed a blatant error.

"Tell me exactly what happened and don't spare me any details." I told him exactly, with repeated emphasis on the suspenders.

"Maybe he found a telegram in his room that contained disturbing news," said my father.

"Maybe," I said.

"Or maybe he was suffering from a disease he never told anyone about."

"Maybe," I said.

"Maybe he suddenly went insane. That kind of thing can happen."

"Maybe," I repeated.

"Stop saying maybe, you jackass, and get yourself to school."

"What should I say when I get there?"

"Anything. Tell them I'm ill and you had to go fetch a doctor."

Maybe the story really did make my father sick. A rigid curtain of horror had spread across his face when I told him. He must have been afraid of losing his remuneration, the roast goose would have been for naught, and new auditors of the Reichenberg–Gablonz–Tannwald Railroad would come and audit like there's no tomorrow. In Old Austria one was used to thinking everything was forever, first and foremost Austria itself, then all of its institutions, especially the Emperor, who, after all, was approaching the sixtieth anniversary of his reign that year, six decades of imperial stability. *"Duodecim lustris gloriose peractis"* had already been prepared as an inscription on the anniversary thaler, and henceforth to eternity! By his suspenders! How was it possible? My father didn't really seem to suffer any personal grief over Herr Pernold's demise, he was more dismayed by the chaos it caused, the disruption to his calculations. The clockwork of his life had suddenly slipped a gear, and the only one within reach was me. So I took his slap in its abstract sense and forgave him on the spot.

The fact that he asked me to lie at school, just like that, really did make me wonder though. When it came to morality my father was a man who went through all the proper channels. "Those who lie, cheat. Those who cheat, steal. Those who steal, end up on the gallows." I knew, of course, that the entire Bohemian Forest couldn't provide enough wood to build all the gallows the monarchy would need. On the other hand, I had to admit that this time he couldn't just say, "Tell the truth!" It was already eight-thirty. How could I have possibly explained to my math teacher, Prof. Gustav Lukas, what all of this meant: Herr Pernold, the Reichenberg–Gablonz–Tannwald Railroad, and suicide by his *Grüss Gott* suspenders? Lukas, after all, was a priori convinced that a pupil would resort to the most fantastic excuses just to avoid a math test. Besides which, Lukas came from Eleonorenhain. "There we can tell right away when someone's lying," he claimed. I would have to try my luck.

"And what flimsy excuses will I hear today?" is exactly how he greeted me when I entered the classroom. "Perhaps the tram wasn't running? Or maybe you had to serve as best man at your grandfather's wedding? Or an attack of gout in your Achilles heel?"

"Beg your pardon, I had to fetch the doctor for my father."

"Is that so? And what, may I ask, is ailing your esteemed father? Hopefully nothing too serious."

"I don't know."

"Well then, I'll have to pay your father a visit this evening, won't I, to see how he's getting along. How convenient that I have an errand to run at the mineral dealer close to where you live."

Lukas, who apart from mathematics also taught general science, was just the type to make good on his threat. And besides, there really was a druggist in Žižkov close to where we lived who sold rocks and crystals on the side. It would have been quite unusual, of course, for a grammar-school teacher to visit the home of one of his students, but this Lukas on his quest for truth was capable of anything, as he himself was the first to point out. "I'm not from some Prčice nor from Napajedla either," he was fond of saying, pronouncing the names of these altogether reputable Czech towns with blatant contempt, "I'm from Eleonorenhain, way down in the Bohemian Forest, where rose quartz is found and people speak the truth." What one thing had to do with the other could have probably only been explained by searching deep at the wellspring of nationalism, which always pretends to have a monopoly on the truth. Whatever the case, Prof. Lukas could have conceivably come, and I'd have to prepare my father and get him to lie, too, to cover up my own falsehood. That would have been the worst part of it. And so, once all the other students had handed in their tests, I approached Lukas in the hallway at the beginning of our break.

"Begging your pardon, sir, I'd like to tell you what really happened."

"How interesting. Now you'd like to tell the truth. And why didn't you do so in the first place? And how will I know if this truth isn't just another lie? So your father hasn't fallen ill after all?"

"No, but Herr Pernold hanged himself."

"Who is Herr Pernold?" asked Lukas sternly, for he sensed I'd concocted a story, without taking into consideration that an invented Herr Pernold is much harder to conjure into existence than a real one. So I told my story with an altogether commendable thoroughness, only leaving out the bit about the remuneration and the slap in the face at the end, since I wanted to spare my father on those two counts and, as far as the slap was concerned, didn't want to degrade myself.

"Roast goose, you say, and by his suspenders. Hmm. A likely story. And that's a reason to miss your math test, this indispensable cornerstone of our educational system? You expect me to buy that?"

Now I was really losing my patience. "Before, you wouldn't believe that my father was ill. Now you won't believe that Herr Pernold hung himself. What *do* you believe?"

He measured me from top to toe, the way people from Eleonorenhain measure people from Prčice. Then he said, "I believe in what can be proven, and not in what I've been told." And with that he dismissed himself.

Great! He believes in what can be proven, and not in what he's been told. That means he didn't believe in anything. Because what, after all, could be proven? Not even what you've seen or experienced. You can imagine this or that, but nothing can really be proven. Only the present moment is able to prove itself. Everything else is a thought, a dream, a story. And even if this Prof. Lukas had personally witnessed the Battle of Königgrätz — a claim my father made for himself, incidentally — that still wouldn't prove to someone else that the Battle of Königgrätz had actually taken place, it would only be hearsay, a secondhand account. America was merely hearsay, Alexander the Great was hearsay, even God was nothing but hearsay. So Lukas didn't believe in God. Apparently all he believed in was Eleonorenhain, and yet he had succeeded in becoming a Gymnasium teacher who decided the fates of human beings. And even with Eleonorenhain, Lukas had to constantly reaffirm its existence in order to keep it alive. He showed us pieces of rose quartz and said, "These are from the area around Eleonorenhain. I collected them myself." That was what he said, what he told us, and we were supposed to believe him. But the suicide of Herr Pernold, this he found implausible. Ludicrous!

In the evening — we were having goose giblets in white sauce, sometimes referred to as the "young parts" of the goose, although no one could explain to me why the organs, neck and head of a goose would be younger than the goose itself, a dish that was eaten with noodles — my father explained to me in so many words: "Women are the root of all evil." Far from wanting to contradict him, I simply asked, "How come?" but all I got for an answer was, "You'll see. How was school?" I told him about Lukas, that I lied at first then told the truth, but left out the part about the remuneration, and that Lukas didn't believe me and might even end up paying us a visit. "Let him believe what he wants," said Father. From work he had sent a telegram to Frau Pernold in Vienna: "Husband killed in accident. Expecting your arrival." Yet another falsehood, because what was "accident" supposed to mean? My stepmother said, "You may as well have told her 'hanged.' She couldn't care less, that woman with her cousin. She'll be knocking at our door tomorrow. Getting on our nerves. Luckily a goose goes a long way."

Just that moment the doorbell rang, and to my horror standing outside was none other than Prof. Lukas. He asked if he could speak to my father. Father appeared at the door.

"I've only come to convince myself of the truth. Your boy missed his test and claimed at first that you were sick. That kind of thing is usually an excuse. Then he told me a fantastic story I was even less inclined to believe. You seem to be in the pink of health, as far as I can tell. So which one's the truth?"

"The truth, Herr Professor, is the fantastic story. My boy only lied so he wouldn't be taken for a liar. But as you can see, the truth didn't do him much good either."

"That's how you raise your son?"

"My dear Professor Lukas, what should he have told you? Fifteen minutes earlier he'd just told me the truth and I slapped him in the face because of it. You expect him, fifteen minutes later, to tell you the same truth? Would you have believed it either? Apparently not. I have to confess it was me who told him to tell you I was sick and needed a doctor!"

"That all seems very peculiar to me," Lukas said, excusing himself. My father had admitted to slapping me in the face. I was proud to have received it.

There were disagreements at breakfast.

"All year not a single guest," my step proclaimed, "and now we have two in three days: a hanged man and his widow."

"A comptroller is a comptroller," my father pointed out, "and the widow of a comptroller is the widow of a comptroller."

"A hanged comptroller is no longer a comptroller."

"But his widow is no less a widow than before."

"Why was she a widow before?" I interjected.

"Shut your mouth," said my father.

"He's right, you know," replied my stepmother, adding: "One goose liver is not enough for four people."

"So make a heart and lung ragout," he answered.

"I'm treated like a maidservant here," she snarled, but since we'd never had one I lacked the *tertium comparationis*. At the homes of my rich classmates, the Reitlers', for instance, I'd seen that the maids wore black cloth dresses, dainty white aprons, and sometimes even lace caps, that they got good tips and had Sundays off. None of which was true in the case of my stepmother. On the other hand, strangers addressed her as "Madam." You can't have everything, I guess.

But Pernold's widow didn't come the next day after all, and the three of us enjoyed the goose liver on our own, the heart and lung ragout being set aside for a future occasion. We didn't hear from Frau Pernold on the following day either. The Prague office had meanwhile informed Pernold's superiors in Vienna and officially requested that the widow be notified, likewise inquiring what to do with Pernold's corpse, which for now was on ice in the judicial morgue. Still, Frau

Pernold never showed. A colleague of the deceased arrived from Vienna, Chief Controller Pohnert, who was supposed to take over Pernold's files and complete the audit himself.

"Another roast goose," my stepmother grumbled.
"Let's wait and see," answered Father, "who knows if I'll even get him to come over and what will become of my remuneration."

Chief Controller Pohnert didn't need to be asked twice. He was less inclined to roast goose and more for larded saddle of hare with cream sauce and cranberries. "At least a change of pace for once," said my stepmother when she heard the news. "Except for the dumplings," I pointed out, "they're always the same."

"There must be something in this world you can depend on," she said. She'd been born in Czech country.

Herr Pohnert was a broad, middle-aged gentleman. He had a dangerous-looking bulbous nose with three dark-red quivering garden strawberries on it. "It was bound to go sour with Pernold, I'm afraid," he explained during the meal. "She — I mean his wife — was not only thirty years younger; to make matters worse, she came from Saxony."

"What's that got to do with it?"

"You say that so lightly. People from different culinary regions should stay away from each other. It only works if they don't care at all about food. And what kind of people does that make them? I once knew a married couple — they'd only been together for a couple of weeks — where the wife, a Northern German, poured dill sauce over a spinach omelet. I was there when it happened. Dill sauce was for beef shoulder as far as her husband was concerned, hailing as he did from right here in Bohemia. But that's not important. It's still part of Austria. Her husband jumps up and says, 'A lousy Kraut dish again?' I thought to myself: Mercy! If he says 'Kraut' and 'again' it must be bad. And I was right, not a year later and the two of them were separated.

Some tramp even ended up killing her. That's beside the point, though you never can be sure."

A thirteen-year-old could learn a lot from table talk like this, even though he was still in shock about the sudden demise of friendly Herr Pernold, which the chief controller referred to simply as "going sour." The boy, for his part, was sorry Frau Pernold hadn't come, tormented as he was by a dimly smoldering memory of her bosom beneath a zephyr blouse, even though his stepmother had remarked in a general way in the kitchen: "When you see that, a lot of things start making sense." What made sense, and why a lot? And yet Frau Pernold, and everything that went along with her, was nowhere to be found. "The apartment on Mariahilferstrasse is locked up tight," reported Herr Pohnert. "The Pernold woman is supposedly out of town. No one knows where. Probably on a pleasure trip again. We'll have to bury him here in Prague for the time being. You can't lie around in a morgue forever. They can transfer his remains later. It's common knowledge he was Catholic."

The dubiousness of the term "forever" dawned on me in all its awfulness. I knew from my real, biological mother that you didn't live forever, but now Herr Pernold had demonstrated it to me once again in no uncertain terms. You can't lie around in a morgue forever. The grave reserved for him had already been declared a provisional one. But if they transferred his remains would the Viennese grave be less provisional? Someday, I'd heard, the graves would open and the dead would be resurrected. Worming your way out of a six-foot hole in the ground is not that easy. I know this from playing cops and robbers, because I'd often ended up in a hole like that since I was always a robber. And when a dead man crawls out of a hole, what then? The Last Judgment, you numbskull, that's what. At any rate, being dead was also not forever. But being alive wasn't either. The only certainty was forever being a numbskull.

Once these fundamentals had grown shaky, I started questioning the basic notions of truth and truthfulness. I told the truth and got slapped in the face for it. My infallible father had ordered me to tell a falsehood and Prof. Lukas rubbed it in my face. Herr Pohnert came for the saddle of hare and was kindly received because of a now uncertain remuneration. Frau Pernold didn't even come to identify her dead husband and specify where he should be buried. And yet she'd been his bride once. I had heard my stepmother, an aging bride, vow to hang together. What a sight!

"Dead is dead," she now declared, "and one piece of earth is just as good as another. Transferring remains doesn't come cheap!" Some nice prospects those were. "So you're basically saying she's right?" I asked.

"I'm not exactly saying she's right, but I'm not exactly saying she's wrong either."

"What does exactly mean?"

"Exactly means not exactly."

Such was the labyrinth of the world the way it presented itself to me. Always right and wrong at the same time. That would mean that even when you were most right you still could not be sure you were right, and even when you were most wrong you might conceivably still be right. "When Herr Pohnert comes to dinner, be friendly to him and don't stare at his nose too much, because he's the one who'll propose the remuneration." As hard as it was for her, even my step-mother managed to be a little friendly somehow. Fiesco's *conspiracy at Genoa*. Stowasser's German-Latin dictionary gave the following definitions of *remunerari*: "reward, return a kindness, give a present, repay, requite." My father conducted the business of the Reichenberg–Gablonz–Tannwald Railroad. What did my friendliness have to do with requital, which sounded more like retaliation? And why would I have laughed at Herr Pohnert's nose? First of all, I rarely laughed.

There was much that was laughable, for sure, but my childhood and its environs didn't give me much to laugh about. Second, if anything Pohnert's quivering bulbous nose was creepy. It could only have been the result of prolonged developments and profound calamities. Like Herr Pernold's suspenders, it was part of the vast labyrinth of the world, in which I had recently taken my first steps and from which you can never return to the paradise of the heart. All you could do was go forward, forever losing your way in the process.

A corridor, then to the right another one, then to the left a third, then a descending stairway, then a steep incline, then another corridor. They say there's a final refuge somewhere. But no one embroidered *Grüss Gott* for me on anything. My stepmother didn't embroider. She knitted socks. Embroidering would have been a sentimental pastime. Knitting was useful and saved money. Besides, if you embroider you need someone to be fond of. Where was my stepmother supposed to get someone like that? She didn't even embroider for herself. Some women embroider, others knit. If someone ventured to object that you can also knit with love, they would have overlooked a crucial difference. Because, of course, everything in this world can be done with love, provided you have it. But you don't embroider without love and necessity. I had an inkling of this even at the age of thirteen. Because that's when you enter the labyrinth in which there's no Ariadne's thread to help you, and turmoil rages everywhere inside you, without even knowing what you're for or against.

Pernold's manner of death had raised some ecclesiastical concerns, but the priest let it go at "paralysis of the heart and lungs" on the death certificate. "What do you want," my father snapped at me, "his heart stopped beating, didn't it? And his lungs stopped breathing." "Yes, but . . ." I tried to argue. "No buts," he cut me off, " 'buts' disturb peace and order." I didn't know how to begin the next sentence, or my life at all, if not with a "but," and so I just kept quiet.

Chief Controller Pohnert delivered a eulogy at the funeral and said the Reichenberg–Gablonz–Tannwald Railroad would never forget its colleague Pernold. My father, the second to speak, said the Imperial and Royal State Railways would always remember him. For no matter if state-run or private, in eternal life all railroads were equal. I was just beginning to contemplate how the memory of an entire railway worked when it started to rain and, before my father could finish, the rain was coming down in buckets on the funeral party. The coffin rested on a bier in front of the open grave, which was full to the brim within a few minutes after the sudden downpour. The few mourners who attended the funeral ran for cover under the nearby trees, which, being cypresses, offered little of it, and from there ran soaking and dripping wet to the main avenue where some maples stood. The two gravediggers were hesitant to lower Herr Pernold into a flooded grave. "He'll wind up floating on top," feared one. "We'll have to weigh him down with stones," the other suggested. Apart from the two of them, only my father and I stood at the graveside in the midst of the pelting rain. We began helping the gravediggers, who decided to do their duty after all, to lower the coffin into the hole and cover it with muddy soil, lumps of clay, gravel, shards of pottery — in brief, to shovel everything within reach on top of it until it was gradually covered and disappeared. When we looked up, drenched and dripping with sweat, there wasn't a soul in sight. If I'd soiled my suit like this playing soccer my father would have given me a hiding, for sure. But now, since his own suit was dirty as well, he merely said, "It was our duty and a good deed." I didn't dare say "but."

The next day, after our natural history lesson, Prof. Lukas asked me how everything had gone. "We buried Herr Pernold at Olšany Cemetery yesterday," I said.

"Excellent," replied Lukas. "Olšany is sedimentary terrain. Nothing remarkable geologically speaking, but superbly suited for a burial ground. Because, mind you, not every soil is equal when it comes to burial purposes. The loamy earth of Olšany, you see, contains various salts and acids extremely conducive to preserving those interred there. After all, there's ample proof that people buried there for six decades, or twelve lustra, can be exhumed, if need be, and are practically unaltered. It's also a proven fact that, even in cases where the wooden coffin has decayed or collapsed under the weight of the soil, the external appearance of the buried person is preserved, and this due solely to the unique composition of this Olšany earth, which doesn't agree with the worms, bugs, and other unwarranted disturbers of the dead and their well-earned peace, which is why this terrain has been a preferred burial location ever since prehistoric times."

"My mother is buried there too," I said.

"You see," said Lukas, approvingly.

Frau Pernold remained untraceable. "She'll come," said Father. "How do you know that?" I asked. "Pension claim," he answered. He was right. A few weeks later she turned up in Vienna. She said she'd been away visiting relatives and knew nothing of her husband's passing. "Fine relatives," my stepmother muttered. Frau Pernold didn't come to Prague. Pernold's belongings were given to her in Vienna. "The suspenders, too?" I asked. "Certainly," said my father, "but she probably didn't keep them. That's not the kind of thing you hold on to."

"So what do you do with them?"

"You give them or throw them away. Or, even better, you sell them to a junk dealer who then resells them." I had the eerie feeling that I was probably doing figure eights on the ice skates of a suicide.

There was naturally no talk of transporting the remains. Frau Pernold received a death benefit and a pension, and my father a thank-you from the board of the Reichenberg–Gablonz–Tannwald Railroad, which continued to keep him in their employ and adhered to the remuneration scheme. With that the Pernold affair seemed closed to everyone's satisfaction.

But affairs of this sort are never closed. They merely conceal themselves for a while, only to reemerge when you least expect it, like the writing on a palimpsest. The entire Pernold tragedy, from the roast-goose dinner to his burial at Olšany Cemetery, had taken place in a mere six days. Outwardly, that is. For it presumably began much, much earlier, in some inaccessible and unfathomable depths of the soul, and continued to smolder afterward. After six wild years of adolescence, it suddenly, for a single minute, thrust itself into the foreground of my life, and it would take another ten times six years before it could be sealed in the present narrative. Sealed? Scattered from here and turned into something enduring. For life is not a fleeting "happening," not a mere chaotic mishmash you can capture with macaronic language or clever metaphors. It can't be tackled from the outside. Its relentless causality demands transparent accounting that registers on its current balance every debit and credit and brooks no attempt at escape.

Six years after that eventful week I passed my graduation exams and set off on a kind of grand tour, financed by a few crowns I'd earned from tutoring. It was enough to get me to Carlsbad, where on the very first day colorful posters enticed me to attend an afternoon gala in the kursaal and later on in the shady spa garden. I sacrificed an entire crown for admission and felt like a grand mogul, since paying this sum entitled me to see a real live archduchess, a niece of the Emperor, who had graciously deigned to open the ceremonies of this charitable event. The famed Kammersänger Werner Alberti would also be performing, the well-known writer Roda Roda would tell a few of his droll anecdotes, and the soubrette Mizzi Zwerenz would perform some numbers from the operetta *Spring Air*. But that wasn't all I got for one crown, even though what the posters advertised seemed to gratify all the senses. The numbered admission ticket was also a raffle ticket for the tombola, whose main prize was a genuine pearl necklace, donated for this purpose by the chairman of the festival committee, one Count Kolowrat-Krakowsky. If you add to this the fact that the one-crown admission fee also included a cup of coffee and a hot Carlsbad wafer (with almond and sugar filling), you have to admit that times haven't exactly improved. Consider, moreover, that this was the first ever entertainment I had enjoyed independently — something I had willingly paid for with my own money, without the pressure of school and exams breathing down my neck, as the master of my own life, in the ambrosial respite between Gymnasium and university, surrounded by a watering place overflowing with amenities, full of elegant visitors from around the world and permeated with the memories of erstwhile celebrity guests, the greatest of whom would determine the fateful course of my own mental world.

And yet the atmosphere of that midsummer day was not entirely carefree and easy. The young man must have noticed this, but it didn't concern him all that much. He knew, of course, that some foreigners had already left unexpectedly, and that others were packing their bags; but a family was speaking French at the table next to him, a bit further he could hear English, and some Easterners in fezzes or turbans had even put in an appearance. What could possibly happen? The hot springs bubbled like always; the light of the heavens shone between the leaves of the chestnut trees trembling in the summer breeze, greeting all things below. The black forests stood mighty. The shouts and warning cries, indeed, even the ominous detonations of that historical period were lost in the majestic murmur of tradition, in the golden waltz-dream rhythms. So what could possibly go wrong? Everything, of course. But all the same, the young man was still full of hopes as he sat there lightheaded and lighthanded on that Carlsbad summer afternoon of July 28, 1914. The archduchess, long and lanky, was solemnly escorted in by dignitaries. The Kammersänger, a profusion of medals pinned to his tailcoat, poured forth onto his listeners in surging baritone: Carl Loewe ballads about Thomas the Rhymer and, more appropriately, about the origins of the folk song "Prince Eugene, the Noble Knight" composed during the Siege of Belgrade. Roda Roda, in a brick-red vest, told slightly off-color jokes with a Levantine flair, which Her Imperial Highness only ever laughed at after a cautious glance at her lady-in-waiting. Zwerenz warbled agreeably, and now everyone left the kursaal to return to their garden tables, where the spa orchestra put on a brilliant show with a medley of Lehár tunes. I sat at the edge of the garden, close to the road, almost an outsider looking in, and shared the table with an older married couple — or so I presumed, because they hadn't exchanged a single word but just sat there motionless like some eerie demons who had done all there was to do in the world and were no longer surprised by anything, not even by the tombola, whose rotating drum was about to be set in motion for the raffle. The neighboring table, as mentioned already, was occupied by some French people, an incessantly chattering family, dominated by the silvery cadences of a ravishing daughter. It certainly wasn't easy for a young man to find himself in such pleasant company, to the sounds of "Vilia, O Vilia! the witch of the wood," counterpointed, of course, by the agonizing realization that the lovely being next to him was altogether out of his reach. The mere existence of this creature was the height of joy and the depth of despair in one. The stiff, gloomy married couple in black must have noticed this, but didn't stir. They sat there like an unrelenting Woe betide you!

Each of us has a classmate we idealized. Since my fourth year of Gymnasium mine was called Hans Gerke, an ever triumphant heartbreaker who had a talent for just about everything, writing poetry too, which for him was just another instrument to perfect the art of living. He surely would have known how to approach the heavenly French girl without even knowing a word of her language. If he'd been there he would have shown me how and, bastard that he was, would have then made off with her. As it was all I had was a stanza he wrote, about a girl who at first seemed unattainable but whom he eventually succeeded in wooing. It was published in the Sunday supplement of the famed *Prager Tagblatt*:

Once I have told you
and none too discreet
about who I am and not what I seem,
then you will stand there and stare at your feet,
and no longer look right through me.

That's how a seventeen-year-old Hans Gerke pictured it, with a baroness no less, the rake, and Karl Kraus in person tore it to shreds in *Die Fackel*, for the lady, much to his chagrin, really no longer looked through Gerke, employing him at her palace one summer to teach her little boys Latin, with all of the consequences. But who else if not Gerke would have managed such a coup? Never in a million years would I have the opportunity to tell this Gallic goddess, and none too discreet, about who I am and not what I seem. And never in a million years would she then stand there and stare at her feet, because she wasn't even looking through me before. My chances with her were worse than with the Mona Lisa, who at least smiled when she looked at you, as I knew from reproductions, even if this smile meant nothing.

Count Kolowrat was now announcing the winning ticket number for the grand prize and the glimmering girl leapt to her feet, waving her ticket and shouting jubilantly: *"Le grand prix! Le grand prix!"* And why in heaven's name not? What in all the world could have resisted the magnetic pull of her charm and grace? Good fortune had to come to her, it was practically made for her, as were the archduchess, Roda Roda, Mizzi Zwerenz, and the whole glorious backdrop of the Habsburg Empire, which now bestowed on her, this radiant creature, a pearl necklace straight from a fairy tale, presented by a count from the ancient Přemyslid line of Bohemian nobles, under the thunderous fanfare of the Carlsbad spa orchestra. She regarded it for a moment, then she curtsied ever so slightly, the count adorned her neck with the pearls and elegantly kissed her hand, as if she had granted him a boundless privilege, at which point I saw her luminous being hover back to the neighboring table, but my head sank before she got there, since I couldn't bear her magical presence, and when I looked up everything was gone, the table next to mine was empty, only the two dark petrified figures were sitting next to me, staring into space. I stood up and took my leave mechanically, but they didn't lift their eyes — symbols perhaps of the eternally unmoving, that which always remains the same regardless of what happens.

The musicians in their temple packed up their instruments, while the waiters began to clear the tables of plates, silverware and scraps of food left over from the celebration.

The signs outside the shops on Alte Wiese were barely distinguishable from one another. I knew a boy who could recite them all in order from memory, even backwards, on either side of the street. That impressed me more than Tasso in my fifth year of Gymnasium. I stood for quite a while before the display window of the mineral dealer, the subdued light of the streetlamps multiplying the twinned crystals, chrysoprases and moldavites, or gently caressing the ribbons in the agate and aragonite. Pentagon-dodecahedron! Bohemian garnets from the Wallenstein region. My long-dead teacher, Prof. Lukas, was good for something after all. "Bear in mind the perpetual enmity between primitive rock and calcareous mountains, the buried oceans in sedimentary rock, and that the Elbogen meteorite fell headlong into the castle well straight from the cosmos, which is why it was called the 'bewitched burgrave.'" Ever since then I had wondered whether it was a meteorite that had turned into a burgrave, or a burgrave that turned into a meteorite? There's a barrier between burgrave and meteorite. Crossing that barrier is called transformation. Once upon a time, I, Chuang Tzu, dreamt I was a butterfly, fluttering hither and thither. Soon I awaked, and there I was, veritably myself again. Now I do not know whether I was then a man dreaming I was a butterfly, or whether I am now a butterfly, dreaming I am a man. Between a man and a butterfly there is necessarily a distinction. The transition is called the transformation of material things.

The streets in the early evening were almost empty now, and the few pedestrians crept and cowered, speaking in hushed tones. The carriages and automobiles of departing guests stood outside the big hotels, waiting to take them to the train station and out of the country. I saw the afternoon goddess descending the stairs of Grand Hotel Pupp with her family, escorted by obsequious porters. Nestled around her neck was a delicately wrinkled veil and below it surely the *grand prix,* for pearls are nourished by the scent of a woman's skin, and now she was carrying herself and all of that away to some marvelous château on the Loire with four bluish helmeted turrets, deep in a garden with endlessly singing fountains. The car, as she got in, seemed to groan with lusty pleasure, shook in erotic shivers, moaned with blissfulness, rattled wildly into motion, and then behind a hazy cloud of exhaust fumes the vision vanished.

I turned around. Which way did I turn? Why did I even turn around? I should have kept going down the old avenue, continued past the gray Posthof and the empty garden cafés, into the night that hung on the mountains, on and on, deep into the Bohemian forests, which would have received me between their bearded spruces, their mossy boulders and bilberry bushes, the high arches of their curly ferns, and cress-lined streams, would have embraced me in their natural fate, freed from human relations, held by clasping roots, pure being. But I turned around and saw in everything the doings of humans, whose fate I, too, like everyone else, had to help fulfill.

It began on the now completely dark street when I noticed in the distance a brightly flickering light and a group of people gathered around a tobacco shop. They were all staring at a telegram stuck to the display window. No one spoke. I wasn't close enough yet to decipher its delicate typescript, because a woman was planted right in front of me, wide and swaying, humming some waltz, a heavy, overpowering scent wafting from her like a veil. It was her — Frau Pernold — after all these years, all the endlessness of my boyhood existence; it was her, or it wasn't her, the epitome of a Frau Pernold, all the Frau Pernolds in the universe, I would have recognized her anywhere in the world. She had one arm linked with an officer's, the other one akimbo. The officer, like some bird of prey, thrust his head toward the telegram and read out loud so that everyone could hear: WAR DECLARED! But despite these two cannon blasts, his female companion kept on humming, kept on swaying, and her macabre scent continued to cast its veil. Then the officer boomed two more words: THANK GOD! And this time, too, the woman swayed and hummed. Fingering with his left hand the golden tassel on his saber, he walked off with a clatter, dragging the singing woman behind him. His uniform may have been Austrian, but I recognized his grinning face from all the illustrated magazines of the world. War declared! Thank God! And on top of it the awful humming and swaying of that woman, who turned her face toward me when she left, the eternal yesterday and eternal tomorrow, transcending time and space.

Which god did he thank, and what for? Yet it served as a prompt for the group to disperse, each going their own way, and all that remained with me was the wearying light shining on two words: WAR DECLARED, and the feeling of utter powerlessness against that supranational officer's grimace, against the insuperable singing and swaying of every Frau Pernold, of all times and places.

And with that I, too, went my own way.

THE ASSASSIN

I can never think of the political lightning bolt of June 28, 1914, without instinctively calling to mind something that happened two years later which would be my peculiar brush with the main protagonist of the assassination in Sarajevo. In the summer of 1916, I was briefly sent by my regimental cadre to the garrison hospital of Theresienstadt. Everyone knows today what this name eventually came to mean a quarter of a century later: a terror center, one of the tragic way stations on the road to the harrowing extermination of countless innocent human beings. But back in 1916, the name Theresienstadt did not have such a gruesome ring. Pleasantly located at the confluence of the Eger and the Elbe rivers, the fortress built in 1780 and razed about a hundred years later was still home to an Austrian military detachment but also to around eight thousand Czech and German civilians who very much felt at home behind the ornamental gates and ramparts, behind the old entrenchments and ditches. In other words, it was actually an open residential town. The fortifications, however, had always served as state or military prisons. The most famous prisoner in olden days was the valiant Prince Alexander Ypsilantis, who in 1821 had attempted with Russian aid to liberate Greece from the Turks but, failing in these efforts, was later held captive by Austria, Turkey's ally, in various prisons, including Theresienstadt. So when I arrived in 1916, the fortress had long had a kind of historical connection to the Balkans and the Levant.

My sojourn in Theresienstadt consisted of waiting and walking in circles. Back then there were all kinds of gardens between the various military structures. One of these was connected to the garrison hospital (which, so I've been told, likewise served as a hospital during Nazi occupation). A part of this hospital garden — or, rather, this courtyard planted with the occasional tree — was separated by an iron fence from another, freely accessible area. But at certain times each day you could see behind the bars of the fence the prisoners being held in the fortress, at least the ones under medical supervision, when they went out for their walk. Someone, without being asked, drew my attention to one of these prisoners the very first day I was there.

"That's Princip, the one who murdered the heir to the throne." It goes without saying that I observed this figure with the utmost attention. He was a wispy young man who walked hunched over, as if his head were filled with lead, his pale, almost bluish face unmistakably marked by the shadow of terminal illness, which he succumbed to not long afterward. I fixed my eyes on him, convinced I could provoke his stare, and it actually worked the third time he passed me, for he suddenly lifted his leaden head and looked me straight in the face. He was no more than two yards away from me on the other side of the fence. Yet his gaze defied expectation, did not have the stabbing look you'd expect from a stereotypical fanatic. It felt like Rilke's panther had grazed me with his glance in the Jardin des Plantes:

> His eyes from passing bars can't hold
> a thing they are so weary.
> To him it seems they're thousandfold,
> behind which all is dreary.

Then he was taken away. From that point on I saw him daily. I would arrive to the minute when the prisoners began their walk. In this otherwise so humdrum town, in which I was forced to await a decision about my coming fate (front, rear echelon or hinterland), I spent my time anticipating the moment that Princip would show up behind the bars and glance in my direction. He did it every time. He seemed to have become accustomed to seeing me stand at a certain place. A curious unspoken rapport had developed between us. I tried to fathom what lay concealed behind his countenance, what constituted the actual human being who'd become the instrument that triggered a global conflagration, if what had happened gave him a sense of satisfaction, and if he even remotely grasped the monstrous consequences of his deed. But when he looked over at me, not the slightest change in expression was visible in his face. I didn't bat an eyelid either. And yet it seemed we'd established some kind of secret contact — a questionable contact, indeed, for behind Gavrilo Princip there was always a pair of guards who kept a watchful eye on him. But the more I tried not to move a muscle, the harder it was for me, so that ultimately I stood before the bars with nothing but a sense of unease, afraid that all of sudden I'd move my mouth or eyes in a way that might be taken as a sign, startling the prisoner out of his torpor and into making a countersign. The consequences for me would have been unforeseeable. And yet over and over again I found myself at those bars, gazing at the assassin.

When I think about it now, I realize of course that it wasn't because he happened to be this particular assassin, but because behind the murder of the prince there was actually much, much more at work than the immediate political objective of taking out that specific individual. Here was the embodiment of a revolt against the authoritarian per se, arising de profundis against the powerful, whose mere existence makes the weak feel oppressed. The Greater

Serbian nationalism of the Narodna Odbrana, the organization Princip belonged to, was merely the midwife of a deeper, intrinsically amorphous rebellion. Gavrilo Princip could have never become an accountant whose greatest deed would be to beget another accountant with the daughter of yet another accountant. Was he Gavrilo Princip at all? He was what the *dramatis personae* of Shakespeare's history plays refer to anonymously as a "murderer." Had this fellow Princip really murdered Archduke Franz Ferdinand? What in fact had risen up against whom?

World history did not so easily lead to the personal and the political. In the grandiose overture to the second part of *War and Peace,* Tolstoy showed that it wasn't really Napoleon and Kutuzov fighting against each other at all, but that massive, mysterious and inexplicable shifts were in fact occurring, first from West to East, then from East to West, just like in the days of yore in the case of the Persians and the Greeks, albeit the other way around. The names Xerxes, Darius and Alexander thus acquired a mere symbolic meaning; a mystic responsibility that far exceeded the individual was concentrated in them. This type of irrationality is always a part of reality, if not its prime mover. Any conception of history that repeatedly attempts to explain reality from the exclusive perspective of material "facts" is necessarily bound to fail, indeed even more so than it would by interpreting reality on the basis of mystic imponderables. For an assassination — and this is true in general — is never the work of an isolated fanatic, a misguided loner, nor merely of a group of conspirators or heroic idealists run amok (as in the case of the tyrannicides, Harmodius and Aristogeiton). The forces at play extend farther back, down into the depths and up into the heights, they comprise the phenomena of an entire era that zeroes in on a single conspirator or hero or madman — call him what you will — who is struck by his fate like a bullet that ricochets off him toward the victim.

Standing in front of that fence, I asked myself how the lone deed of this broken creature walking behind those bars and now turning his eyes toward me could in any way be linked to the monstrous, worldwide ramifications and chain reaction of catastrophes affecting all of humanity. An eminent Jewish sage, Shmaryahu Levin, once spoke to me in Prague of an astonishing Talmudic legal provision. Accordingly, a Sanhedrin should not condemn a man if it is so unanimously convinced of his guilt that there isn't the shadow of a doubt. In this case, the extent of what has happened exceeds the capacities of earthly justice, which, given this oversized guilt, should entrust it instead to the judgment of God. Incidentally, this is not just a Jewish line of reasoning but one that was widespread in antiquity. It's a notion that has often preoccupied me, and I've always linked it to the words of the apostle (Romans 6:14) that humanity lives not by law but by grace.

The last time I stood at the fence — I didn't know it would be the last time — someone behind me said, "That's Princip. They should've hanged him." Evidently the person who said this believed he knew what earthly justice was. He thought he knew better than the Talmudic judges, and better than Emperor Franz Joseph, too. He was sure that a man named Princip had murdered an archduke by the name of Franz Ferdinand. He was utterly imbued with the notion that he himself was in no way involved or complicit in this event. And he let it go at that. For in his mind the world was simple. Indeed, the world was very simple. He was also convinced that he or his kind would one day be called to lord over it.

A NIGHT OF TERROR

My evening visit to Café Arco was completely harmless in nature, yet scarcely half an hour had passed before I found myself on the run, fleeing up the stairs and through the corridors of the old Prague apartment building whose ground floor housed the coffeehouse. Here's what happened.

During the First World War, I served for a spell as a soldier with a special detachment in Prague. Off duty I was allowed to wear civvies. I was also permitted to live in private quarters — in this case, with my father. Even so, it was forbidden for me to be out after nine in the evening without a special permit. One December evening, at about twenty to nine, I was on my way home when I passed the coffeehouse and saw Werfel, Kafka, and the blind writer Oskar Baum sitting at a table behind the broad picture window. I went in and joined them, not planning to stay very long.

We spoke about far-flung topics, and not about the war. I remember exactly that we talked about the letters of Abbé Galiani and about the famed Quesnay, who had coined the maxim *Laissez faire, laissez passer*. The time passed quickly, and I hadn't noticed it was a quarter past nine when suddenly the headwaiter, Poschta, came to our table and gently whispered: "The military police, gentlemen. They're already in the next room."

"Get out of here, fast," Werfel told me. "They might catch you." He knew what he was talking about. "Or do you have a permit?"

I didn't, so I got up and walked as inconspicuously as possible to the lavatories in the back. I knew that from there a little door led to the hallway of the apartment building, where I thought I'd be safe. Not having a permit would have meant at least two weeks of confinement to barracks and, if the commander was in a bad mood, possibly even being sent to the front.

When I passed through the lavatories, Weissenstein, the world reformer, came out of one of the cubicles and, buttonholing me, said: "I just read a wonderful article by Herr von Hofmannsthal in the *Insel Almanac* about heroic deeds and glory." Needless to say I wasn't too curious about the contents of said article at that particular moment, so I wrenched myself away from the danger of a literary lavatory conversation and quickly slipped into the dark corridor. Just to be on the safe side, I climbed up two flights of stairs and waited. I thought that after a brief interval I could go back down then make my way home. I had to be in uniform and report to my detachment early in the morning.

I waited and listened in the dark. For a while all was quiet. I was about to go back down to the coffeehouse and grab my coat from the cloakroom when suddenly I heard voices coming up the stairwell. It must have been the military police, who had gone the same way as me through the lavatories.

I hurriedly crept up to the third floor, where the family of my former Gymnasium classmate Kraus lived. I rang the bell without a moment's hesitation, and an instant later the housemaid opened.

"I'm a friend of your young master," I whispered. "Let me in, fast. I have to hide for a while from the military police."

"But the young master isn't in."

"For heaven's sake, don't talk so much. The police are downstairs in the hallway already. Let me in."

"And me too," whispered a second voice behind me.

There was no time for lengthy debates. The girl quickly grasped the situation and sympathized with our predicament. A few seconds later we were in the entrance of the apartment and could hear the voices of the police on the stairs.

"Turn out the light and be quiet."

The entrance was separated from the stairwell by only a single door with a frosted-glass window.

"There's no need to be scared," I whispered to the girl, "we'll leave in a few minutes, as soon as the police are gone."

The girl was Czech. She was surely not on the side of the Austrian military authorities.

The pursuers had now come up the stairs but walked past our door while we listened with bated breath from inside. They climbed up to the fourth and fifth floors, then they came back down, stopped on the landing outside our door, conversed back and forth while my heart stood still, then went down the stairs to the entranceway of the building. The danger seemed to have passed.

"Let's just wait a little bit," I said softly, "until the coast is clear. Is Frau Kraus home?"

"She and the young lady have been asleep for an hour already in the back bedroom. The young master is on duty in the hospital at the Straka Academy."

"I know. Let the ladies sleep. We'll be out of here soon enough. Where's the phone?" I wanted to check with Headwaiter Poschta at the coffeehouse to see if the military police had gone yet. Luckily the phone was in the front hall. "The gentlemen from the police are still here," reported the waiter in a low voice.

"We're going to have to stay a little bit longer," I said to the girl, whom I could see more clearly now, the light from her room reflecting off her. She had flung a dressing gown over her shoulders. She didn't seem apprehensive. "Perhaps the gentlemen would like to go to the drawing room in the meantime," she said. "We can turn on the light there," she added.

I was hesitant at first. I knew Frau Kraus. I didn't doubt her goodwill. But taking her hospitality for granted, unasked, at this hour of the night seemed a bit presumptuous to me. On the other hand, the whole thing couldn't possibly last much longer. So we quietly entered the drawing room, myself and the other man — the one who had slipped in with me. I turned on the light. The room was freezing. December 1916.

I took a good look at the man. He was in uniform. His rank: platoon commander. A lean man with sharp but almost benign facial features. "Hoch- und Deutschmeister Regiment No. 4," he said, referring to Vienna's home regiment, "but here without leave." That certainly could have cost him dearly.

"I'll make some tea," said the girl, who'd followed us in. "The missus won't notice a thing." The girl was very young and had a twinkle in her eye. She seemed to be enjoying this unexpected nocturnal adventure.

"Nonsense," I said. "No need to make tea. We'll be out of here in no time. I'll call the café again in a few minutes."

The Deutschmeister sat down in a rocking chair. "Sit on the sofa instead," I said to him, "the rocking chair creaks. Frau Kraus might wake up." He obeyed. He didn't tell me his name, and I didn't tell him mine. We were silent. I knew the drawing room well from visits long ago. Like most bourgeois parlors — usually called the "salon," and only entered on special occasions — it contained an array of plush furniture. There was a glass cabinet with porcelain figurines, antique cups, and colorful Bohemian glass. Pride of place in the bookcase was held by the magnificent Brockhaus encyclopedia. On the wall hung a large heliogravure depicting Brahms at the piano, also a reproduction of a doctor making a house call to a visibly tubercular girl, and finally an etching by Heinrich Vogeler-Worpswede with a virgin sitting in the middle of a field of flowers. The print was called *Spring*.

After a while I returned to the phone.

"The messrs. from the military police are still here," reported Poschta. "I don't know what's the matter, but they won't go away."

Just as I was hanging up, I again heard in the stairwell the same heavy footfalls of several individuals. They came up to our floor again, and I saw their lantern lights sweep over the pane of frosted glass in the door to the apartment. Again they stopped and conferred with one another. I listened, motionless, but couldn't understand a word. Finally they proceeded up the stairs only to come back down after a while, passing by our door and continuing downstairs. I breathed a sigh of relief.

"It looks like we're in for a long night," I said to the Deutschmeister. "The police are still here. They seem to be onto something."

"Well then, we'll wait it out," answered the Deutschmeister, who spoke in a German dialect I can barely imitate. The girl made us tea after all. She even brought some pastries, a luxury in wartime. Then she lit a fire in the tall tiled stove and was going to sit down with us. "I'd go to bed if I were you," I said discourteously.

"I wouldn't think of it, this is far too exciting."

"Maybe for you. For us it's lousy. We have to wait till these fellows disappear. Who knows how long that'll take."

"It's true," echoed the Deutschmeister, "you can't never tell."

The thought that Frau Kraus might wake up for some reason and suddenly enter the room made me pretty uneasy. She might get a sudden headache and come looking for a Pyramidon tablet. Or maybe she'd awake from a symbolic dream and want to look up something in the Brockhaus. There are countless reasons for a woman to get up and suddenly enter her drawing room. If she did, she would find two men drinking tea with her maid in the middle of the night. Before I'd even have a chance to explain this bizarre situation, she would let out a bloodcurdling scream and the military police would burst into the room and lead the two of us away. Any explanation would be futile, and we could count on the worst.

At times I managed to calm myself down. This quarantine couldn't last forever. It was already past eleven o'clock. At some point these sbirros would get tired and go away. I called the headwaiter again, but again his reply was negative. He was reliable. I had told him where I was. He knew me well. I always paid my tab, and never omitted even a single pastry when splitting the bill at the table. I hadn't mentioned the Deutschmeister, though.

Time passed. The girl, gauging our mood, presumed she'd no longer be needed and finally went to bed. Her calmness in the face of two total strangers, and men at that, in the middle of the night, was certainly remarkable. Midnight came. The coffeehouse was closing now. I wouldn't be able to call anymore. From now on we were left to our own devices. Several more times I heard the policemen walking up and down the stairs and on the landings.

The Deutschmeister had stretched out comfortably on the sofa. He may have only been a platoon commander, yet a little silver medal for bravery was gleaming on his uniform. "Strange, all the places you end up spending the night," he observed. "I'm from Tyrol."

"Nice place," I said.

"Yeah, Tyroleans are a merry lot."

"That's what they say."

"But you know what, sometimes they can get pretty wild," he added.

"No harm in that," I said reassuringly, "it happens everywhere."

The drawing room was meanwhile toasty warm.

"Speaking of getting wild," the Deutschmeister said, resuming the conversation, "something happened when I was in Tyrol just a while ago."

"What's that?"

"Something really bad. This guy I know killed his girl in the village."

"That's awful. How'd that happen? And why?"

"Well, he came from the front, on furlough. You come back from there with all sorts of notions in your head."

"What kind of notions?"

"Well, take this fellow, you wouldn't believe it, he's a farmer's son like me, a decent kid like me. Goes to church on Sunday. His father has twenty tracts of land and five head of cattle. They requisitioned seven from him. They've got a few pigs, too. And what did he have to say about the front? I'll tell you one of his stories, just to give you an idea. They were marching through the forest, somewhere in Galicia, and he shot and wounded a Russki. The guy was lying on the ground badly wounded when he got there. The Russki pulls out a picture and shows it to my friend, a photograph of a woman and child. He couldn't even speak, or maybe just Russian. So he holds up the picture and begs him to have mercy, to let him live. And what do you suppose this friend of mine does? He stabs him with his bayonet and kills him. Just like that. You see, those are the kind of notions you bring back from the front."

"Terrible," I said, "what war can do to people."

"Ain't it? Makes you wanna cry. And the thing with the girl."

"What happened with the girl? Was she cheating on him?"

"Far from it! A faithful girl, she was. Pure as low-dust flour. You can take my word for it."

He meant a lotus flower. "Didn't love her?" I asked.

"Of course he loved her. He would have had himself drawn and quartered for her. Would have pulled the sky down for her."

"So why did he kill her?"

"Nobody knows. Probably not even he knows. He came home on furlough. Spent six nights in a row with her. I'm telling you, a girl as true as gold. On the seventh day, when it came time to go back to the front, he stabbed her to death, just like that. Those are the notions people have nowadays."

He was silent, and I didn't know what to say either. I looked at the delicate girl in the Vogeler-Worpswede etching.

"Look," he said, resuming our conversation, "take our case, for example. What war can do to people, you said. Well, you don't have a permit and I don't have leave — that is to say, mine's expired. But that's not a crime. We run like rabbits and try to hide, that's how scared we are. You had a black coffee, I had a black coffee. I saw you, by the way, in the coffeehouse downstairs. And what are you now, all of a sudden? A criminal, that's what you are. If they catch us they'll put us in the clink. They turn you into a criminal, like it or not. Did you want the war, by any chance?"

"No. I definitely didn't want a war."

"You see, there you have it! Did the Russkis want the war? Nope. Did the Frogs want it, or the Limeys, or the Krauts? The wops sure didn't want it. You're not gonna tell me that somebody wanted this war. And now everybody's in it, slaughtering each other. Believe me: one war begets another."

"What was the medal for bravery for?"

"Medals? Don't even ask. I don't even know why I got it. I shot and shot and shot, then I ran straight ahead, then I shot some more and ran straight ahead again, even shit my pants in the process and puked like a sparrowhawk. And then they gave me a medal, for 'valiant conduct in the face of the enemy.' That's what they call a hero, in case you didn't know. I think I'm gonna sleep a little until this mess is over." He stretched out his limbs, yawned profusely and, turning over on his side, fell asleep and started snoring.

The snoring made me nervous. The menacing noise of a saw cutting through complete silence could have easily carried to the back room and perforated the sleep of Frau Kraus. This had to be avoided, so I nudged the Deutschmeister.

"Don't sleep. You snore too loud. You'll wake up the ladies. Things could get pretty awkward then."

"True enough," he said good-naturedly. "I'm just tired as heck. But I wouldn't want to cause any problems. Who lives here anyway?"

"The husband is a doctor and is at the front. Their son has also reported for duty. He's a schoolmate of mine. The mother and daughter are here, though."

"Well then, we don't want to disturb their sleep now, do we. It's good that we can be here at all. Those goddamn police. Nothing but a bunch of shirkers. I tell you, if those fellows come in here I'll give it to 'em like they've never seen before."

"You'll do no such thing. That's just what we need. You'll land me in hot water."

"Right again. I was just saying. Actually I'm gentle as a doe. I never did wrong by nobody. Never took anything from no one. I always told myself: you're just too nice. Once I even pulled a man out of the Inn River in winter, saved his life. Of course it was me who threw him in when we were fighting, 'cause we happened not to be friends. But I pulled him out all the same."

"So it turned out okay in the end."

"Sure did. I was lucky that time. You can't always be that lucky. That other fellow, for instance — I mean the one who did his girl in — he wasn't so lucky. Some things you can fix, others you can't. That's how it is. She was a very pretty girl. Rosl was her name."

"I'll go have another listen," I said.

I closed the door of the drawing room behind me so that no light could reach the entrance and fall on the frosted-glass window of the door. The maid was apparently sound asleep in her room. Not a creature was stirring. All was quiet in the stairwell and the entrance, too. Maybe the policemen had gone after all.

It was probably safe to leave the building through the main entrance now, but of course that would have meant waking the janitor, which would have been rather conspicuous at three o'clock in the morning. And walking the streets of Prague at night would not have been very prudent in my case, because military police were patrolling there as well and could have easily stopped me, and that would have been even worse than if they'd caught me earlier in the evening in the coffeehouse. It was better to wait it out until morning, at which point I could hurry home, throw on my uniform and try to make it to six-thirty roll call. Reporting sick was not an option; at sick call and in the military hospital they would have pegged me for a malingerer in no time. I had to get out of this mousetrap somehow, and no later than five-thirty.

There was silence all around me, but now and then something creaked. Every sound is amplified when it's dark, and your hearing improves when you can't see anything. It was creaking here, creaking there. But then it stopped. Then all of a sudden I heard footsteps and voices coming up the stairs again, saw light and heard, "Karo, over here . . . Karo, there . . . !" They seemed to have a police dog with them.

I broke into a sweat. Now they were at the apartment door, just a few yards away from me. I stood motionless and felt myself trembling. I heard the dog sniffing. But they passed like ghosts. Then I heard them on the fourth floor, knocking on a door, heard loud voices and an exchange of words, then it went quiet again. I waited. About ten anxious minutes later they returned, talking while they walked past our door, then went down to the entranceway. They might have had what they were looking for now. But there was no way of knowing for sure, so I snuck back into the drawing room.

"Well, how'd you come out?" asked the Deutschmeister, which I took to mean: what did you find out?

"Nothing. They came back, went into some apartment on the fourth floor, then went back down again. They even had a bloodhound."

"You don't say! A bloodhound. Well, I'll be damned! I suppose they've got their man by now."

"Maybe . . . Maybe not."

"What do you mean, maybe not? With a bloodhound? But you could be right. I tell you, they're capable of anything, they'll haul in the most innocent people just so they can say they arrested somebody."

"How do you know the fellow on the fourth floor is innocent?"

"Right again. Nobody is completely innocent. Everyone's done something. At least something little. I always say, everyone's involved. Everyone single one of us. You can be sure of that."

"Just a while ago you said that nobody wanted a war. And now all of a sudden you say it's everyone's fault. That doesn't make sense. Personally, I feel pretty innocent."

"You're mistaken there," philosophized the Deutschmeister, "I don't mean the war's their fault, but in general. I wouldn't want to question you — pardon my saying so — about how many times you chose to say nothing, and all the things you allowed to happen that didn't need to happen. I tell you: everyone's involved."

"If you look at it that way, you're probably right."

"You see," he said, content. "But don't you worry, you ain't no worse than the rest of us."

"Thanks," I said, "I'm relieved to hear it."

"Tell me, what's your military rank? You can't be much if you need a permit."

"Ah, I'm just a titular lance corporal."

"You don't say! A lance corporal. And a titular one at that. Then you'll have to stand at attention before me. But you're the college type of course, a university man."

"Yes," I confessed, "in civilian life I write for the papers."

"Aha! So you're an editor. You flunked out of college. Pardon my saying so. I always heard that's true of most editors.

"People tend to exaggerate," I said, but I wasn't about to discuss with him the reasons for getting into journalism.

"Well, maybe someday you'll write a nice story about this unusual evening. You'll have to send it to me — that is, if I can still be reached."

"Why shouldn't you?"

"You never know, do you," said the Deutschmeister, pensively. He was silent for a while.

"So why come to Prague from Tyrol?"

"What do you mean by that?" he said in a huff. "Oh, you mean why I've come here all the way from Tyrol. It's like this. I wanted to visit an uncle here. But he moved away. Spent a few days looking for him in Bohemia. You haven't got a chance with the folks around here, let me tell you, you're just another stone in the road. No one knows nothin'. I drank a Pilsner in some little joint. That's how I overstayed my leave. Is that really a crime?"

"Heavens, no! I thought we agreed on that one."

"And anyway, criminals. What's a crime, I ask you? Someone who plucks a flower 'cause he wants to stick it in his hat, or who picks pears 'cause he finds them tasty — does that make him a criminal? The criminals are the ones who chop off the roots at the stem."

"Depends on who the flower or tree belongs to."

"Well, would you look at that! Next thing you'll be quoting the

Civil Code or stories from the Bible. But let me tell you: stealing means taking something from someone who has a right to it. But first you have to prove to me this person has a right to it. Just look at all the things going on at the front. You have no idea! And afterward they make a big fuss 'cause someone pockets something that someone else doesn't even need and doesn't have a right to anyway."

I was hardly in the mood to develop a moral theory of property or to explain to the Deutschmeister how the transgression of property rights might conceivably be a transgression of the very core and existence of humanity, nor did I want to argue with him that the abolition of property rights is only conceivable in a perfect Kingdom of Heaven. I had other problems at the moment. The Old German pendulum clock was tenaciously ticking in its cabinet, and time was passing.

"The girl he killed," he continued after a while, "it was suicide, if you know what I mean. Not because they might hang him later. He's dead already, before they can even catch him. There's no point hounding him and chasing after him. The noose is already around his neck. He took God's business into his own hands, and that's not a good thing."

"You didn't want to hear about the Bible a minute ago and now you're talking about God yourself."

"Ah, you and your education! Don't you see that someone who takes God's business into his own hands doesn't believe in God? As a child, sure, you believe in God. Later you lose interest. Just yesterday, for example, I was walking in the park by the train station and a little boy comes runnin' up and asks me, 'What time is it?' The boy was German. Normally they're all Czech around here. 'Aha,' I said, 'they've corrupted you, too, with their hours and minutes. Probably don't have a permission slip, huh?' 'What do you mean, corrupted with hours and minutes,' says the boy, 'the time is what you read on a watch.' 'Yes,' I say, 'but who made the watch?' And you know what the boy said? 'The watch,' he said, 'was made by the watchmaker. But the watchmaker was made by God.' I almost cried, and had to buy myself a slivovitz. That picked me up a little."

It was meanwhile almost five o'clock, and something had to happen to put an end to this situation. Not only was my roll call approaching; the danger that Frau Kraus might wake up was growing by the minute. I secretly devised a plan. I went into the hall and tapped on the door of the maid's room. "Please, get up and get dressed, quickly." I heard her puttering around, and a few minutes later she was standing in front of me.

"Take a shopping bag, please, and go downstairs as if you wanted to go fetch something. Then check to see if the coast is clear in the entranceway."

The girl came back shortly.

"The coffeehouse," she said, "is open already. Some customers are sitting inside. But there are two men who look like undercovers standing in the entranceway of the building." She was prudent and had bought some bread at a bakery that opens very early, thus giving her an alibi. "Luckily I still had some ration cards left, and I know the baker woman."

My only option now was a fairly risky escape. I knew that the café owner Suchánek lived on the first floor, and that a spiral staircase led from his apartment directly down to the coffeehouse.

"Go out one more time," I asked the girl, "go get something else. Go through the main entrance of the coffeehouse and up the spiral staircase to Herr Suchánek. He knows me. Give him my card — here. Tell him that I'm here and have to get out. Be fast. Tell him to give me a sign from the first floor, a little cough, so I know it's okay for him to let me through his apartment and into the café. Just make sure the policemen in the entranceway don't notice anything." The girl's eyes sparkled. She left immediately.

"Where did she go?" asked the Deutschmeister.

I explained in a few words what I was planning to do.

"Not a bad idea," he said, "he just needs to let us through, the café owner." Are you sure he's not in cahoots with the police and won't pull one over on us?"

"I don't think so. He's a decent fellow."

"Well, it don't really matter to me one way or another," said the Deutschmeister with resignation in his voice, "I'll have my problems sooner or later."

After a while he continued: "You know, a night like this is actually rather pleasant for the likes of you and me. A warm parlor, good company. You can get a few things off your chest . . ."

"I can imagine something more pleasant," I interjected.

"Because you're still young," he said. "Later you'll find out that a friendly conversation is the best thing a person can have. Look, the two of us are sitting here together. Just yesterday we were complete strangers, and now we're kind of like good buddies, don't you think? Nothing tops a little friendliness."

Nope, there really is nothing better, I thought, while listening anxiously for a sign from the first floor.

Then, after a painfully long time, I heard the sound of a throat being cleared. I signaled to my companion in misfortune, and we both slipped quickly and silently down two flights of stairs.

Herr Suchánek stood in the doorway of his apartment, wearing a long nightshirt. Strange, how the most trivial details are imprinted on our minds in moments like these. The nightshirt was white, with patterned red-and-white trim along the collar and sleeves. Suchánek looked at me. He looked at the Deutschmeister. He made the sign of the cross.

"Not him! Not him!" he whispered in Czech, "He's a murderer. Jesus and Mary! I'll lose my license!"

The Deutschmeister seemed to grasp the situation instantly. He made no attempt to force his way in. In a matter of seconds he had taken off his uniform coat and the gray sweater underneath, then put the uniform coat with the silver medal back on and the sweater on top of that. He now looked like a civilian. In a flash he opened a window on the landing. With a single bound he vanished into the lightwell, where dawn was beginning to break.

Suchánek, who was trembling all over, let me in and — by way of the spiral staircase — into the coffeehouse, which by now was filling up, located as it was right across from the train station. I went to the cloakroom and grabbed my coat, which had hung there unnoticed all night, and ran home in double time.

My father, who had heard me coming, began to lecture me. "Where were you all night? Which skirts were you chasing? How could you in times like these, when men are dying on the battlefield . . ."

"Father, I beg you, don't hold me up now. I'll explain everything to you later."

"What's to explain," he ranted on, "you're acting like a good-for-nothing."

I went about my duties rather absentmindedly that day. I was free from five in the afternoon on. The first place I went to was Café Arco, the way an offender inevitably returns to the scene of a crime.

"They nabbed that fellow," whispered Headwaiter Poschta in my ear. "On the roof of Toufar's, the pork butcher, that's where they got him. The police had been looking for him for days. Supposedly for murder." I quickly paid for my black coffee and rushed to the Straka Academy, where the son of Frau Kraus, my former schoolmate, served in an emergency hospital.

"I have to tell you something," I said. "Sit down, and don't be scared. I spent last night with a fugitive murderer in the drawing room of your apartment."

My schoolmate Kraus smiled incredulously.

"It's not a joke," I said. "The man's been caught now. I'm telling you this just in case he tells them where he spent the night. Your mother knows nothing about it — and shouldn't know anything, either, unless it's absolutely necessary."

I described the dramatic *nocturno* for him. "Hopefully Anna will keep quiet," he said, "and hopefully that criminal won't spill the beans either."

"Hopefully," I murmured, and had an eerie feeling. Harboring and concealing a wanted felon was a serious offense. Frau Kraus could have gotten out of it. But as a soldier in the Austrian army I would have been in deep.

The girl-killer Albin Strohberger admitted during police interrogations that he'd spent the night in the lightwell, on the glass roof of the coffeehouse lavatories. He stuck to this statement even though they claimed it was impossible because the lightwell had been searched several times. They couldn't get anything out of him and finally let the issue drop, deeming it irrelevant.

I was relieved.

A few weeks later, my schoolmate Kraus invited me to afternoon tea at his mother's apartment. I didn't feel too good about it, but felt I had to accept. We sat in the drawing room. I took a seat in the rocking chair.

"Why don't you sit on the sofa instead," said Frau Kraus. "The rocking chair creaks so unpleasantly."

I looked at the green plush furniture, the glass cabinet, the bookcase with its opulent Brockhaus, and the etching by Heinrich Vogeler-Worpswede. "You've got some nice old Bohemian glass," I said.

"Yes, they're from Haida," said Frau Kraus. "The nicest is this cameo glass, look, with the inscription: *A good conscience is a soft pillow.*"

The girl brought the tea. She served it with an expressionless face. Then she left the room.

"What do you say about the little episode that took place in our building?" asked Frau Kraus.

"What happened?" I asked in reply, acting as clueless as possible.

"What? You don't know? The incident with the murderer. It was in all the papers. Just imagine, that monster was hiding in our building all night. The police were even here, with a bloodhound. They forced their way into Broneck's on the fourth floor around midnight. The dog was pawing at their door. They searched every single room. Frau Broneck nearly had a stroke. They even opened all the cupboards and cabinets. Imagine how scared the Bronecks must have been. And the confusion. Goldstein, Lady Broneck, you know what I mean."

The girl entered the room again and silently served us cake, which looked like a Sacher torte but was actually a wartime substitute made with sugar-beet syrup.

"All night long that murderer was in our building," Frau Kraus continued. "And we were sleeping away in the back bedroom. We didn't hear a thing. You didn't hear anything either, did you, Anna?"

"No," the girl answered, "not a sound. The man said he spent the night in the lightwell. The papers say he confessed to the murder. Of his beloved. Will they hang him?"

"Surely," said Frau Kraus, "what else are they supposed to do with him? He must be a terrible brute." The girl stood there for a moment, indecisively. Her gaze met mine for a few brief seconds. I think that never in all of my life have I looked at a girl with such gratitude. Then she took the tray and left the room in silence.

ONE LAST DEED

One cheerful morning, barely two weeks before I left my native city for good — presumably for good — I met in one of the many little nooks of Theingasse a man of middle years who clattered over the pavement with a peg leg, carrying in front of him a cigar box full of matches and shoelaces. This person played a peculiar and, as it turned out, very important role in my life.

I knew him from childhood. His name was Svatopluk Janda, and he shared a desk with me in primary school. Even back then he was missing his right leg, having been hit by a streetcar in a careless moment while playing ball. Since then he hobbled on his wooden replacement, which earned him a certain respect, bordering on adulation, among his six- and seven-year-old classmates. Rather than being depressed or gloomy, he tended to be feisty and domineering. And his unusual physical strength, not impaired by his missing leg but apparently enhanced in his remaining limbs, even made him feared.

I attended a German school in the Prague suburbs where almost all of the children enrolled came from poor families. The son of a low-paid official, I was nonetheless considered wealthy and pampered, even though my daily allowance was a mere two kreutzers. When I asked my father to raise it to three, he replied by way of explanation:

"Who do you think you are? I'm not made of money and I don't shit ducats either. One kreutzer more a day would be three florins sixty-five kreutzers a year. In ten years that would be more than forty florins, with interest and compound interest. You think I can spare forty florins just like that?"

"But, Father, you drink a glass of beer every day, and a liter of beer has gone up one kreutzer . . ."

"That's a different matter altogether," explained my father. "Beer is liquid bread. And, anyway, don't get fresh or you'll be in for a surprise."

A "surprise" in such cases, I knew well enough, meant a couple of slaps in the face.

So this is what my wealth amounted to, the reason I was despised rather than envied by my classmates. Svatopluk Janda despised me the most. He despised everyone, actually, our teacher Petrak included. Svatopluk was reminiscent of Long John Silver, the villainous one-legged pirate from *Treasure Island*. He could sling his schoolbag with such momentum that it knocked its target flat on the ground, and the expression in his dark-brown eyes would sometimes become so menacing and sinister that no one, not even the teacher, dared to contradict him. There was nothing malicious or mean about him. He only ever got dangerous when he sensed some kind of injustice. Maltreated by fate in his early years, he of course had a keener sense of injustice than the rest of us. Under Svatopluk's guidance, we soon realized that the world was a much more unjust place than we'd imagined.

For four years I sat in the same classroom as Svatopluk. Then I went to Gymnasium, an upheaval much more momentous in my case than the transition normally tended to be. Because, coming from an environment of poor children toughened by hardship, I suddenly found myself in a neighborhood and institution that was full of mostly rich mama's boys, with silk scarves tied around their necks to protect them from drafts and satchels containing well-packed ten o'clock snacks — thoroughly sheltered children from well-to-do families. If in primary school they'd disdained me as "the rich boy," in Gymnasium — at least at first — I was scorned for being "the poor boy." My fellow pupils in primary school had at least invited me to their homes, which were crammed with countless objects hoarded for some unknown future purpose. I would later notice that the rich households seemed empty by contrast, and even later still that they're always slightly boring, old-fashioned and absurd.

I lost track of Svatopluk Janda for more than three decades after primary school. Of course I thought of him from time to time. I saw him next to me at our double desk, his wooden leg propped horizontally against the drawer, his alert and twinkling eyes roaming around the classroom; I saw him before me playing catch in the schoolyard during recess, how he moved with remarkable dexterity, to the admiration of those around him; I saw him during fights, how he packed a powerful punch, dealt out lightning-like kicks with his wooden leg, and took down any opponent with unexpected holds and moves; I heard him reading out loud from the third-grade primer, a highly memorable passage that was supposed to point out the difference between related terms:

The minister has a consort.
The director has a wife.
The postal clerk has a spouse.
The worker has a missus.

I saw him forming a chain with the others and doing a ghastly round dance around me, while everyone bawled:

Ha-ha-ha,
Where's your mama?

(Actually, I had no mama at all, just my step. Anyway, at home my classmates never said "mama," just "mother.") I saw Svatopluk Janda before me, on a hill behind the Fliedermühle (an inn on the outskirts of town, not far from school) making out with a girl his age. He was the first of us to hang out with girls. We learned all kinds of things from him. He was the son of a day laborer who drank more than he worked, and of a mother who had to keep an eye on six other children and therefore had no time to be psychoanalyzed. Svatopluk survived the streetcar accident as if through some kind of miracle. The question is moot if his parents were pleased about this. For four school years I had him next to me on a daily basis. Then, for three decades, he only crossed my mind occasionally.

"Janda," I said, "Svatopluk! How are you?" By the look of him, there was no need to ask. He didn't reply, either, just looked at me for a while with the same dark, uncanny eyes. He scrutinized me from my suit down to my shoes.

"I know," he said, "you're the rich kid, Urzidil."

"Oh, knock it off. I'm not rich. I never was rich. You guys just imagined it."

"So you're not rich? Maybe you're just wearing a disguise, and you normally walk the streets like me, selling shoestrings and matches?"

"Well, not exactly," I said, embarrassed. "But only by sheer chance. Still, there's a huge difference between a rich man and me."

"Is it as big as the difference between you and me? Answer me! Is it as big as the difference between you and me?" Lightning flashed in his eyes, and I cowered as if he might kick me with his peg leg.

"Maybe you're right," I answered, sheepishly. "But it's really not my fault."

"That's possible," he reflected. "Besides, you're a dimwit, and you've probably got a cushy job because of it."

I ignored this comment. I'd known a lot of stupid people with pretty substantial incomes. And I'd often suspected that it couldn't actually be all that hard to rake in tons of money, given the earnings of certain people whom I knew for sure were certified imbeciles. Incidentally, I was not so sure of my own intelligence at that point in my life. So I didn't answer. But I also didn't dare pull out my wallet and offer some money to Svatopluk. It didn't even occur to me that my talking to him like this in broad daylight must have seemed conspicuous to passersby or even to people I knew. Perhaps — I'm ashamed to admit — I would have avoided such a conversation at a different point in my life. But in those days, the final days of Old Prague, when life as we knew it was breaking down, things had become a little different.

"Can you do lunch with me?" he asked, thus relieving me of my embarrassment. "I like to eat," he added with a wink.

"But of course," I hastened to say, "of course. Me too. Where should we go?"

"To my place, obviously," he said. "I live nearby. A dandy like you can't be seen in a restaurant with me. Especially since I have a criminal record. You mind?"

"No. Of course not. I mean, nowadays a lot of people . . . Hold on a minute. I'll go buy a few things."

"Buy things? No need. I've got enough at home. I have bread and loads of sausage. But it's horsemeat. Have you ever eaten horsemeat sausage?"

"Horsemeat sausage? I don't think so."

"Well, there we go. And you say you're not rich. You haven't even eaten horsemeat sausage. Let me tell you, it tastes better than you think." He hobbled his way forward through narrow Theingässchen, where not many people were out now at lunchtime. He stopped in front of one of the little old houses, pushed the door open with his elbow and led me into a dark, stuffy hallway, at the end of which some basement stairs led to a room whose only source of light was a low, grated window, a blind one at that, looking up into a courtyard. "Don't be alarmed. It's cozy in here," he remarked. "But in Pankrác it was a little better." Pankrác meant the Prague prison, named after the neighborhood where it's located. Svatopluk's place did indeed resemble a dungeon. (It reminded me of *The Count of Monte Cristo*.) It had a sour smell, like old garbage. It gave me the creeps, but I pulled myself together. Svatopluk lit a small kerosene lamp and I could now make out how the room was furnished and the walls with their plaster, half of which had fallen off. I recognized a bed made of shoved-together crates with a few ragged horse blankets and a bulgy drill sack, presumably stuffed with rags and serving as a pillow. A larger crate was used as a table, two smaller ones served as stools.

Old plates, glasses, a tin can, and a few indefinable objects wrapped in newspaper stood on a three-legged trestle table dubiously holding its balance.

"A fine accommodation," declared Svatopluk. "I've lived in worse. Like I said, in Pankrác it was a little better."

"Why did they lock you up?" I asked.

"Ridiculous question. Because I took something once that had no value to anyone but me."

I didn't ask for the details.

"It's like this," he began on his own. "People like you don't understand that kind of thing. People like me will always be punished for theft, sooner or later. Generally sooner than later. You can't steal anything from us, so we have to be the ones who wangle something out of the others. Clear as boot polish, isn't it?"

It was hard to argue against this logic. "Is there no one to help you?" I asked. "You must have brothers or sisters."

"Yes, I do. But help me? Two of them are still around. Vlasta has four children out of wedlock. She could use my help. And I've got a brother too. Fantastic! He's a railroad employee and won't let me near him. Get lost or I'll end up losing my job, he told me. You want a schnapps?"

"Thanks, I don't drink schnapps," I said prophylactically, although this wasn't entirely true.

"That's good," he said, shaking a bottle of kümmel, "'cause there's none left."

The horsemeat sausage had a metallic, iridescent shimmer on the cut end and tasted sweetish. The bread was dried out. I ate, because not for anything in the world did I want to displease my host, much less incur his wrath. I felt like I was in the cave of Polyphemus, anxiously awaiting what would happen next. Svatopluk ate large chunks of sausage, heartily and in silence. I noted with horror that his left hand was mutilated too.

"A beer would be nice right about now," he said when he finished eating.

"I'll go get some," I suggested.

"No need. I'll get one for us. That is, if you pay. 'Cause I don't have any money." I handed him my wallet, which he opened with his right hand. He studied its contents, shook his head, took out the amount he thought he needed, and handed the wallet back to me. Then he hobbled to the door.

"Dobrohlávková, beer!" he called into the hallway. "Money first," a rattling female voice echoed back. "Greedy bitch," growled Svatopluk. He dragged himself out and came back shortly with a bottle in his hand. "She even took a deposit for the bottle. She's got a stash at home. She doesn't go to the pub. And I don't for sure. Nusler beer. You drink Nusler?" I said yes. He took a big swig then offered the bottle to me, after wiping the neck with his sleeve. I drank.

"A real feast today for once," he said, contented. "Just like St.

Matthew's." (St. Matthew's was an annual fair in Prague.) "I've got some pickled onions, too, from my purveyor to the court who runs Café Candelabra on the square."

(Café Candelabra was a sausage stand parked under a lamppost on Old Town Square. The sausages were rumored to hold a race in your stomach, an indication of what was used to make them.)

"You remember Petrak, the teacher?" he began after a while. "A decent fellow. I ran into him a few times later. 'Janda,' he said, 'can't you help yourself at all?' 'How should I help myself,' I said, 'with just one leg?' 'But you've got two hands,' he said. 'You could get some kind of work. I'll get you a job in a factory.' He actually did. And I even showed up. That was twenty years ago. And this is what came of it."

He waved his left hand in front of my eyes. Two fingers were missing.

"How did that happen?" I asked.

"It happened, that's all," he said. "I saw the two fingers fly from the gearwheel. They flew through the air like woodchips. Whoosh, and they were gone. They paid me a couple of crowns. My own carelessness, they said. Petrak, the teacher, also helped me out for a while. Then he died. A decent fellow. But he gave me bad advice."

"He meant well."

"Meant well? Of course he meant well. You should leave people alone, though. You can at least give the ones who don't mean well a kick in the pants. But there's nothing you can do to save yourself from the well-meaning ones. They're so well meaning it ruins you."

I preferred not to defend people's good will, at least not in the present circumstances. Svatopluk had stretched out on his crate-bed. "And what kind of nonsense have you been up to?" he then asked.

I couldn't give him a straightforward answer. At the moment I had no profession. I was lucky I couldn't tell him anything. Any mention of a steady income or some kind of occupation would have only made him bitter, if not furious. At the time I was on the verge of fleeing the country however I could, without yet knowing how I'd do it.

"I have to get out of here," I said. "I mean from Prague or, rather, the whole country."

"Aha," he said. "You're probably one of those politicals. I've heard about those things. Well, that's none of my business." He sat up, contemplated me for a while, then said: "There you go! You probably didn't do anything wrong. You've probably never even stolen a lousy hundred-crown bill. No, you don't look very capable to me. And still they won't leave you alone, your own people."

They certainly weren't my "people," but I kept quiet.

"You see," he continued, "your own kind! And they won't even leave you alone. I've at least got a home. Nobody can chase me out of here. I'd like to see the fellow who tries! I don't have to run away from anyone." He looked at me hard. "You really seem like a poor devil to me. Well, if you need anything let me know, I'll help you. I can still turn a few tricks with my eight fingers. I don't have any money, though . . ."

"Janda," I said, "if you need money, I mean for yourself . . ."

"Don't you dare," he cried, "you need it more than me, you jackass. No offense." He got up, went over to the three-legged table, and unwrapped one of the bundles in newspaper. "This is my archive," he said. "I want to give you something. I've got something for you from our schooldays."

"What? After thirty years?"

"Yep. Strange, isn't it? It just gets lugged around with me. Here, a paper of yours. Petrak made you write it once. 'Return with your father's signature: I shall not talk or whisper in class.'"

It really was a piece of paper on which I was supposed to write said commandment twenty times in a row. But my father's signature — I remembered well — was forged. Petrak, the teacher, noticed immediately of course, and summoned my father to school. "Signature forger!" my father screamed and smacked me in the face, "Signature forgers — the worst thing on God's earth!" I was ten years old at the time.

"Why did you save this scrap of paper?" I asked, astonished.

"Why? You whispered the answer to me, and you were talking to me. Petrak threw it away afterwards and I picked it up. I don't know why. I've had it ever since. And now you have it, as a keepsake. Back then you had balls at least." I took the paper and tucked it away.

"There you go," said Svatopluk. "Everyone has something for someone. Now it's time for a snooze." He stretched out on his makeshift bed again. I got up.

"If you need something, just stop by," he called out after me, and it seemed that never in all my life had I received a more sincere invitation.

I marveled that someone could take a nap in that oppressive phase of the German occupation. Nightly sleep, too, had been condensed into a very short time span. It was rare that someone fell asleep or woke up of their own free will. Fear is the basest and most deplorable state of mind and spirit, and arousing fear to achieve one's aims is the worst crime against human dignity. For fear, even in its subtlest manifestations, is the first step to insanity. This is ancient wisdom. The Savior himself established these degrees of the soul.

"You have heard that it was said to those of old, 'You shall not murder; and whoever murders will be liable to judgment.' But I say to you that everyone who is angry with his brother will be liable to judgment; whoever insults his brother will be liable to the council; and whoever says, 'You fool!' will be liable to the hell of fire."

I spent little time at home those days, because home meant being where they could find me, exposed to the clutches of danger. I avoided the main streets when I was out, because many people who knew me and who now served the new authorities could have run into me and eventually betrayed me. But the side streets also entailed risks. I spent time in the apartments of others, but they weren't any safer than I was, indeed, my very presence may have only put them in greater danger. They, too, were startled when the doorbell or the telephone rang. When alone, you sought company; and as soon as you were with others, you wanted to be alone. You went to people who you never would have gone to before, to the most fleeting acquaintances, just not to be at home. Home no longer existed, it changed from hour to hour. One night, when I was leaving from such a visit, they were taking someone away from a neighboring apartment. The light in the stairwell reflected off the polished jackboots of this black cohort surrounding the man as they lumbered down the stairs. He looked at me but I stood there, immobile.

I went to cemeteries. In the labyrinth of tombstones and mausoleums you were most likely to go unnoticed. The army of dead people, those who had suffered it all already, had a calming effect on me. I accompanied strangers on their last journey, stood with mourners at these strangers' graves as if I belonged to the funeral party, and probably tossed a shovelful of earth onto their coffins as well.

I went to cinemas, where for two hours you could be anonymous between a few hundred people in the dark. Mickey Mouse playing tennis. Bicycle races in Denmark. Whale hunting with Eskimos. Henry VIII eating a roast, which he holds in both hands, greasy gravy trickling down his brocade sleeve. He'll behead one of his wives when he's done.

How to get out of the trap? Thousands waited naively, in long lines in front of office doors, for permits they would never get. Some fought their way across deserted mountain slopes, through border forests, or even through mines whose shafts ran to the other side of the border. Others swam across border rivers, and still others swindled their way through the border using false papers. Quite a few were caught and brought back with malicious triumph. Some came to grief along the way. Others were too exhausted to even make the effort and ended up taking their own lives. All around, to grotesque rhythms, whirled a gruesome dance of death. Some sought refuge in madhouses. Whoever makes a fool of his brother shall be liable to the hell of fire.

Together with others you evoked the past; or you told ancient jokes, longing as you did for distraction and amusement. Said our Greek teacher, Prof. Komma, once: "Bäumel, aren't you the brother of Friedländer in the fourth form?" Even better: "Komma to Bäumel: You excused your unpreparedness yesterday with the sudden illness of your grandmother. Well, I've made some inquiries. And I discovered, to my great consternation, that the dear lady, thank goodness, is in the pink of health." Burst of laughter. The elevator is running outside. Anxious silence. "Does anyone know another Komma story?" The elevator passed, not stopping at our floor. "My nerves are shattered," says the lady of the house.

Fear gave rise to the most ludicrous calculations. The illicit trade in false passports proliferated in coffeehouse restrooms. Family jewels, securities and other valuables were handed over to complete strangers. Those who wrote letters had agreed on a secret code with the recipients. The letters were like Dadaist poems. "The briefcase is in the boiler . . . The cat is in the sewing machine." That basically meant: My husband got out but they nabbed my daughter. Anyone hoping to escape tried to learn foreign languages fast. *"Mr. Brown is proud of his greenhouse . . . Mrs. Brown has an inkstand." "Nous sommes à Paris. Voilà le tombeau de Napoléon! Voilà l'école de Berlitz!"* Maybe it would come in handy. Tragedy wore the mask of absurdity. Comedy was dressed up as tragedy. Many packed their suitcases and promptly sent them abroad. As if the house were on fire, they randomly grabbed the most abstruse things and put them in their bundle. Silver candlesticks, pointless paperweights, framed flower-pieces on glossy paper fashioned from the hair of an elderly aunt, with the inscription "In remembrance" (likewise made of hair). Others imagined they were being particularly clever by putting old copper-plate engravings in their suitcases. Chodowiecki! They say he's much in demand in America.

You tried to flee — not only from the impending violence all around, not only from the tyranny of injustice, but also from the chiliastic madness straight from a Hell Brueghel canvas. Where was there a place untouched by this witches' sabbath? Not even the churches were immune. I see my old friend Alfred König before me. It was in the Church of St. Nicholas in Lesser Town. I had entered not exactly out of piety, but to isolate myself from the agony of the outside world in the quiet of this sacred place. I tried to pray. It had only occurred to me to pray when I saw Alfred kneeling in a pew before me, his head resting on his folded hands. He was a man of sincere faith, who had joined the Church late in life but did so with fervent conviction. He was a writer, and had authored a number of works on Church history after his conversion. We had once spent many evenings together, and I'd always admired him. When I saw him kneeling and praying, I thought he might be one of the select few who lived in a state of grace and had found their way and their truth. Overhead arched the gigantic baroque dome with its hovering gloriole of saints and martyrs, to whom his quiet prayers seemed to rise along the rays of light that fell obliquely and steeply through the windows. And so I, too, began to pray. "Thy kingdom come." Then I saw two men approaching Alfred from behind, one of whom lightly tapped him on the shoulder. Alfred got up, as if this tap on the shoulder was something he'd long been expecting. He was about to walk off with the two men when his eyes met mine. He had bright blue eyes. In that split second all the suffering and all the compassion of existence seemed to merge in those eyes. Escorted by the two men, he walked away through the rows of pews and towards the bright opening of the portal, into a light and into a darkness he would never return from again.

I no longer went to churches either. There was only one place I knew I was safe, where the times couldn't reach me.

I didn't mind that half the plaster on the walls had fallen off. It gave the walls geographical ornaments. One spot looked like Arabia, another like South America. And at the bottom right you could clearly see the Falkland Islands. Looking at the wall reminded me of some doggerel I'd written in my school days.

> I'm shaken by the world map, its swirl of states a wondrous sight.
> Parallel lines denoting plains. Alpine ridges flashing white.
> Blue are the oceans, yellow is Mongolia,
> Ice-green Hudson Bay, rust-red Anatolia.
> Bull fights in Seville, blubber bars where Eskimos shiver,
> Tea from Iceland moss, lianas on the Amazon River,
> I'm everywhere at once, and never do I tire,
> Through all the many latitudes extends my glorious empire.

Svatopluk, who indulged a good deal in the kümmel I'd brought, constantly bawled a chorus from *The Bartered Bride*, evidently his favorite tune, a folk song everyone was singing:

> Let us rejoice, let's be merry
> While the Lord grants us good health . . .

"Look here" he shouted, "am I not healthy? I've got a bum leg, and half a hand is gone. But otherwise I'm fit as a fiddle."

The hole in the basement was really rather cozy this time.

Svatopluk had pushed the drill-sack pillow underneath me. On the crate-table he'd even laid out some plates and alpacca silverware inscribed with "Hotel Monopol."

"That's *my* hotel," explained Svatopluk. "Red Zimmerhackel is the chef there. He gives me a whole heap of grub twice a week. Today it's meatloaf. You remember Red Zimmerhackel?"

I had to admit that I'd completely forgotten him.

"But you know Red Zimmerhackel," cried Svatopluk in amazement, "the one who tripped the school inspector. A capital fellow! Everyone called him Red Zimmerhackel."

He took a whole pile of meatloaf slices out of their newspaper wrapping, as well as unpacking from another piece of newsprint the bread, sausage and pickles I'd contributed.

"Now all we need is beer and cigarettes," he said, looking at me inquisitively. I handed him my wallet.

"But I have to invite Dobrohlávková today," he added, "otherwise she'll be offended. Today's her day. Whenever I get back from the Monopol."

Frau Dobrohlávková's rather weathered face did at least show traces of her former charms. Her frizzy, peroxide-bleached hair had grown in dark brown at the roots. Her otherwise lean body was interrupted by a massive and aggressively ostentatious bosom that swayed back and forth autonomously with every one of her ceaseless movements. Her face had a smiley expression, without it being certain if she really was smiling.

"If it weren't for me, Svatopluk would have long since perished, let me tell you. Who takes care of his stuff? Who keeps order? Who procures things? If it weren't for me . . ."

"Shut your trap," interrupted Svatopluk, "and don't talk trash."

"Trash," cried Dobrohlávková, indignantly, "everyone needs order once in a while. But all he cares about is food and booze. Me, I'm completely different. My father was . . ."

"I know exactly what your father was," interjected Svatopluk, "I did time with him at Pankrác, six months."

"That was a misunderstanding," objected Dobrohlávková. "It was only out of friendship that he acted as a lookout. He didn't do anything wrong. He was duped."

"That's what I mean," shouted Svatopluk, "getting locked up without having done anything, that's quite a feat. And a Růžička on top of it."

(The Růžičkas were a vast family of tinkers who roamed from place to place in Bohemia and Moravia, as well as in Slovakia.)

"My father was a craftsman," protested Dobrohlávková. "He patched up a broken pot so well you could cook in it for another ten years. I've still got one of them. And my mother was a famous spiritualist."

"She could read coffee grounds," explained Svatopluk.

"That's not true. She foretold the future in a person's palm," screamed Dobrohlávková, enraged. "Everyone knows you can tell a person's fortune from the palm of their hand, everything's there, past, present and future."

"Stop jabbering about palms," said Svatopluk, flaring up.

"I'm stopping already. But true is true. I'm a spiritualist too."

"Especially when you drink kümmel. That's your spiritualism," said Svatopluk.

"You should talk," she said dismissively, taking a big gulp to wash down a slice of meatloaf. "My mother even foretold Countess Chotek's future back when she was still very young. Just don't travel, is what she said. It could turn out badly, Miss. Don't ride in an open car. You might have trouble, Fräulein. You just stay home. And you see what happened?"

"What happened?" I asked, absentmindedly. "What happened? Good heavens! They killed her in Sarajevo, that's what happened, in an open car, together with Franz Ferdinand. That was the start of all this turmoil. And who predicted it? My mother."

There was a brief silence, like at a funeral service.

"Yep, those were the days," said Svatopluk then.

"What do you mean?" asked Dobrohlávková, confused.

"Well, that those were the days, that's all," said Svatopluk. "These days just aren't the same."

"You mean because there's more turmoil?"

"I wipe my ass with your turmoil. That stuff is for people whose lives are way too comfy. Tell us something funny instead, so we have something to laugh about. She's a good storyteller. Tell us a story. But a true one."

"What do you mean, true? Everything I say is true." Dobrohlávková crossed her legs and lit a cigarette. "Which one would you like to hear? Maybe the one about the Kralowitz geese. Have I told that one already?"

"You tell it different each time. And each time you say it's true."

"It is, too. So the Kralowitz geese it is. That was before the story with the Chotek lady. I was a girl of thirteen at the time. There used to be geese by Kralowitz, at the edge of the forest. Whenever we passed by the geese would follow us. One day the Kralowitzers came running up and shouted, 'You stole our geese!' But that wasn't true."

"Must have been some truth to it," said Svatopluk.

"It wasn't true at all! They followed us on their own, all the way into the woods. The Kralowitzers drove the geese back into the village, cursing all the way. And we continued to Roslowitz. We had a covered wagon with a nag called Cossack. My mother could predict the future from his whinnying, especially on New Year's. The next day the Kralowitz geese were back. Geese know where they belong, you know. But some Roslowitz geese had gotten mixed up with them. So the Roslowitz peasants came and hollered, 'Hand over the geese!' We yelled back that some of them are Kralowitz geese. The Roslowitzers shouted, 'They're our geese, and you're a goddamn pack of thieves!' They went and got the village constable, and my father said they should go to Kralowitz, then they'd see that it wasn't just Roslowitz geese. The constable left and came back with the Kralowitz cottagers, who were looking for their geese but couldn't find them in the gaggle. We said: 'It's not our fault if the geese run after us.' The Kralowitzers and Roslowitzers began to yell and fight about the geese. The geese cackled and hissed in between. One of them flew on top of our wagon and wouldn't come down. They called it and tugged at it from both sides until our horse, Cossack, got skittish and bolted, along with the wagon and the goose. By the time we caught up the goose had vanished. The constable let us go, since they couldn't prove anything against us and we really were innocent. But the next day the goose was suddenly back in our midst again."

"I believe it," said Svatopluk.

"Don't interrupt me," said Dobrohlávková. "The goose was with us again, but not for long. Because my father said: 'Before you get us locked up we'd be better off roasting you!' What else were we supposed to do with the goose?"

"Naturally. That's your father, alright. Innocent as a babe in the woods," piped in Svatopluk.

"Either you want to hear the story or you don't! So we plucked the goose, packed it in clay, and ran a skewer through it. That's the proper way to roast a goose. The geese like it. The clay gets hard as a blast furnace, the goose gets evenly browned inside, and the juices stay in it. The goose was almost done and we were smacking our lips already. Just then the constable appeared, sniffed around and said, 'What are you roasting there? A stolen goose.' My father said, 'We're not roasting a stolen goose. It's the goose that followed us yesterday, then disappeared and came back today.' 'It's not your goose, in any case,' said the constable, 'and I'll have to confiscate it.' What were we supposed to do? My mother said, 'Wait at least until the goose is done roasting. A half-baked goose is useless.' The constable saw the sense in that, so he waited until the goose was cooked and my mother knocked the clay crust off with a rock. 'You should try it,' she said to the constable, 'you've probably never had anything this good.' The constable didn't want to at first. But it smelled so good that he couldn't resist, especially since my mother had cabbage and dumplings in the kettle. The cabbage, I will admit, we'd taken from a field along the way, but the flour for the dumplings, upon my soul, as sure as I'm alive, my father had gotten from a peasant in exchange for repairing a bowl. The constable devoured almost half the goose. Then he said, 'It's better this way. Because we don't even know if it was a Kralowitz or a Roslowitz goose.' 'It doesn't matter now,' said my mother. And she predicted his future for free into the bargain."

"What was his future," I asked.

"Oh, the usual. The way futures are. It's not so hard to predict the future. What happens to people that's so out of the ordinary? They come together, they separate. Everyone has their misfortunes or sometimes even good luck. If he drinks too much cold water, he ends up with a belly full of lice. And if he tells the truth too much, he gets hit in the mouth with a fiddle bow. If you take a good look at people, you can tell what's going to happen to them. You just have to mix up the black and the white enough. Something is bound to be right."

"And what do you predict for me?" I asked.

"First you've got to put a five-crown coin in your hand."

"Don't let her con you," warned Svatopluk.

"That's just like him to say such a thing," burst out Dobrohlávková. "That's what I get for always helping him out. Who gets you your matches and shoestrings? And who even brought you a dozen pencils not so long ago?"

"Not so long ago? I've been carrying them around with me for three years already."

"And you have the nerve to complain on top of it! You're sitting too pretty! Instead of being happy that people give him money and don't even take anything."

"What do they take from you when they pay?"

"They always take a piece of me. Always a little piece, believe me. Now then, show me your hand. We can do it without the five crowns."

"I believe it," said Svatopluk.

Frau Dobrohlávková studied my hand.

"Well, what can I say? Maybe you'll be lucky and make a long journey. But things might also turn out very badly for you. An awful lot can still go wrong. Don't make so much of yourself, then not so much will happen to you. The smaller the grain of sand, the more powerless the steamroller."

"Enough of your words of wisdom," growled Svatopluk.

"I have to go anyway," she said. "I have to make my rounds." She shot a scrutinizing glance at me. "You're lucky your head isn't on a woman's body," she said, and left.

"I should actually go now too," I said to Svatopluk.

"Where to?" he asked.

I wanted to say: "Home," but couldn't bring myself to say it. The word had become so meaningless that my lips had no reason to form it. I stayed with Svatopluk. It was homey and peaceful at his place.

"As far as I'm concerned, you never have to leave," he said, stretching out on his bed of crates. "Funny lady, that Dobrohlávková, with her stories. She's got a nice Gypsy quality to her. The story with the geese, for example."

He started laughing, and I laughed along with him.

"I'm happy to hear you laugh," he said. Then he turned to face the wall, and almost instantaneously his chuckle mixed with a snore that gradually gained the upper hand, becoming more and more regular.

I watched the flickering of the kerosene lamp whose chimney was half-blackened by soot, and listened to this deep, carefree snoring in the midst of a silence interrupted only now and then by the bells of Týn Church. Once I heard voices coming from the hallway, probably Frau Dobrohlávková returning from her rounds with someone or other. Then it was quiet again, and the only sound was Svatopluk's snoring like the rumble of water in a canyon.

My gaze got lost in the geographical shapes of broken plaster. I saw the prairies and the Rocky Mountains,

> saw the steam of virgin forest
> and the curly smoke of wigwams,
> heard the roar of massive rivers
> and the thunder in the mountains.

One of the last and hence best deeds one person can do for another is simply to make them laugh, bringing deep relief from their burdens and afflictions. Another good deed is to help a person discover that there are always places capable of withstanding even the most relentless onslaught of historical events, an asylum and refuge for those who still have the strength to perceive the insignificance of all that has accumulated on the core of being, the iridescent layers that have caused this core to be forgotten.

A restless day after the previous night had me running between the nets, sometimes invisible but always palpable, cast across streets and squares and through time. Only those who knew the secret passageways slipped through. The city, like so many things back then, had become more medieval than ever; suddenly it had ramparts and gates that had to be passed through. That the best among us were forced to use deceit and deception as a weapon of last resort was perhaps one of the deepest forms of degradation in those days.

You have to make people laugh — or cry. Only then are they human and true. The ones you had to save yourself from, they were beyond crying; their tears had long been leached out of them. So what about laughter?

The train rolled out of the station, and the shadows of familiar buildings now collapsed for good. Who, when I'm not there, will sing the song of the buildings and alleyways, the late flash of sunlight on steeple knobs, the musing caryatides; who will capture the quiet hum of old ladies selling pretzels in the park, the fates of both riverbanks, the grandeur of its bridges? The train worked its way through the night toward the border. I knew this borderland: its gentle mountains and maternal woods, the slopes that lay there black now but whose colors were so familiar to me, and that now, like every year, were getting ready for summer. Sleep settled heavily in the valleys. Who, when I'm not there, will fathom the golden burst of morning buds, the cry of the thrush and the sparkling quartz? Who will celebrate the wild rustling of the wind in the treetops and the endless downpours, who will unravel the branching club moss on the forest floor, commune with the chicory, and follow the copper-colored beetles? Rest assured! Someone will do it. Many will do it. Who are you, after all?

The train jerked to a halt. It was three in the morning. The border! At this time of day, even the most stubborn border official might be drowsy. At this time of day he might not notice that something isn't right. That's what I was hoping. But he might be in a terrible mood because of his night shift, especially strict about everything, and nasty to everyone he deals with.

"Border control! Exit permits!"

I reached into my pocket and took out my documents. The official was an older man. He glanced at the papers.

"What? You call this an exit permit?" He noticed. Now I was in for it. "Yes," I said with assumed firmness, "that's the permit I was issued."

"Your head must not be screwed on right," he said. "I shall not talk or whisper in class? What's that supposed to mean?"

Terrified, I looked at the piece of paper.

"Excuse me," I said, "my papers must have gotten mixed up. Something from an old scrapbook." I searched my pockets. "Here's the exit permit."

The official's eyes lit up. "Of course, that's the one we need," he said and started to laugh. "I shall not talk or whisper in class — I had to write the same thing myself once, fifty times, that kind of thing happens all the time," and he shook with laughter until he was crying, while placing the stamp on my forged exit permit. "I shall not talk or whisper in class! Can you believe it! In the middle of the night!" And he laughed his way into the corridor.

The train started moving. The border receded behind me, and the night detached itself from the things around me.

The sun came up and changed colors in the usual way. I glanced in the only book I'd brought with me. "Who is this that darkens counsel by words without knowledge? Where were you when I laid the foundation of the earth? Tell me, if you have understanding. Who laid its cornerstone when the morning stars sang together and all the sons of God shouted for joy?"

The train pushed forward into illuminated plains. Half-timbered houses sprang up and passed by; roads crept up and darted off into the unknown; people and carts inched their way into the day. Everything was alive all around me.

"Have the gates of death been revealed to you, or have you seen the gates of deep darkness?"

With that I closed the book.

STEP AND HALF

S he was a stately woman in the turn-of-the-century sense, tall, with a full head of black hair and a piercing dark-brown stare that betokened sinister things to come for the heart of a boy who had lost his mother. The seven-year-old was awestruck by her ample forms, the appeal of which he would only later begin to fathom, as he racked his brains to figure out what could have led his father to pick this particular woman.

The first time she appeared the boy was down with the measles, in the late summer of 1903, a sunny afternoon hung over the suburban street. From the bed he saw the pigeons on the window ledges and the sharp profiles of the stucco decorations on the buildings across the street. She attempted a few nice gestures, one has to grant her that (the only time she ever did), and brought a set of Anchor Stone Building Blocks, purchased secondhand, along with three oranges. Yet the boy could sense they were not really gifts but were actually meant as bribes. Then, a few weeks later, they told him: "You've got a new mama!"

And so there was a wedding, with liver-rice soup and aromatic chives, roast goose with cabbage and dumplings, and sweet yeast rolls in a wine custard called *Chaudeau* (but pronounced "chateau"). That was all fine by him. Some wine for the boy, too, half a glass, just this once. Drink a toast! They took a fiacre to the new apartment.

An older building, overlooking a courtyard, second staircase, third floor, with a long gloomy hallway, the kitchen facing the courtyard, a machine repair shop below. The conjugal bedroom (conjugal bed!), two mighty bedframes right next to each other, nightstands on both sides, finely polished, with chamber pots inside, and looming above it all, the Sistine Madonna in a gilt frame. Green plush sofa with a balustrade over the backrest, lined with porcelain bric-a-brac: rococo cavalier bowing to the right, rococo lady curtseying to the left, shepherd and shepherdess. A three-legged table made of bamboo sticks, leafy plants on top, two wardrobe giants, Fafner and Fasolt, a Petrof upright piano with "Maiden's Prayer" between two twisted candles. Trumeau mirror up to the ceiling.

The boy's room. Keep it clean and don't make a mess! Do your homework at the little table by the window! View: part of a railroad bridge, part of a railroad embankment, part of a dark arched opening underneath. He once saw a girl there with a boy. This gave him sleepless nights and dark circles under his eyes (that and the noisy bed next door). Toys, discarded by acquaintances: a rocking horse with no ears from Herr Krasa (Personnel Director, first name: Hannibal); tin soldiers from Frau Hübscher, paint mostly peeling, legs bent; tin train from Herr Gottstein, known as "old Gottstein." Say thank you.

First Christmas in the new apartment. A tambourine with shuttlecock from his step (the kind of thing girls play with, phooey!), a gun from Papa (pull the trigger and a ring wrapped in colored yarn flew through the room). Action at a distance. First shot he fired hit the rococo cavalier and sent it crashing to the floor. Irreplaceable! Slap in the face. Fight. Who buys that kind of trash anyway. His gun? Hit the porcelain cavalier? Slamming doors. You, off to bed! Crying in the pillow. Oh, golden childhood!

Slaps in the face aplenty, but only from Papa, from the right and from the left, none of them undeserved, it must be said. It's wrong to think the boy hated his father for it. They benevolently ordered the cosmos, and what's more: he was slapping his only child in desperation. His father has to be defended against his step. She never slaps faces; she gives dirty looks.

It was the time of the Russo-Japanese War.

From Port Arthur
Comes a cart,
On it sits Admiral Kamimur'

sang his step, who was Czech by birth and hence rooting for the Russians. The boy and his father were for the Japanese and despised General Kuropatkin. These were the two factions in Prague back then. "Ha-ha-ha, General Kuropatkin victoriously retreats," roared his father over the paper. "Ha-ha-ha, victoriously retreats," howled the son, thumbing his nose at his step in a display of solidarity. Whereupon his father whacked him on the head, just for form's sake, which the boy fully understood.

Father and son walked through town to houses of worship and taverns. Catholic, Protestant, Russian Orthodox churches, synagogues, old and new. "Have a look," said his father, "have a listen," adding in a mutter: "None is worth more than the others!" They wended their way between sights and sounds, glittering gold and choirs, litanies and mumbled prayers. The taverns, though, were all different from each other. There was Pilsner at the Golden Cross and Konopischter at the Cowshed, Smíchover at Glaubices' and black beer at Fleks'. (His step always just drank a small one.) Some very entertaining people came to the beer garden at Fleks': the radish women and mandoletti vendors, women selling pickled onions and silvery rollmops, and men with candied fruit lined up on sticks and neatly piled on top of each other, the lottery men and the ones with electrostatic generators. And then there was the military concert on Shooters Island in the middle of the Moldau, which wasn't bad either with its renditions of the "Radetzky March" and "Heavenly Aida."

Time passed at home with the usual quarrels and truces until one day his step unexpectedly badmouthed his mother. He stared at her and his hands began to twitch. He only had vague recollections of his mother, from when she was on her deathbed. He yelled at his step and threw his full cup of coffee at her, which flew right past the tip of her nose and shattered against the doorjamb. Prudently she didn't say a word to his father about this little incident. The boy was also terribly ashamed. From now on, though, they were mortal enemies.

His animosity was always on guard, in every dream, thought and action. It accompanied him on his way to school, sat next to him at his desk in the classroom, raced alongside him up the hill in the afternoon when he played with other boys, smoldered over the dinner table, rustled in the bedding. But she wasn't all bad, his step, it should be said in fairness. She was a first-rate cook, kept everything spotless, was always lugging things morning and night, was obsessed with doing laundry, was a paragon of thrift and avoided any unnecessary expenses. In a word, she was loathsome even in her virtues. She bickered and quarreled with his father when he came home tired from the office, even though as the father he was always right. The boy thought long and hard about how he might get back at her. Maybe put salt in her coffee when she wasn't looking. Or Seidlitz powder in her chamber pot. Skirmishes of this sort ended with slaps in the face from Papa. Fair enough, since, after all, as a husband and a father he was in both camps.

His step had two old portraits of her grandparents hanging in the drawing room, a full-bearded scribe and a bonneted baba. So the boy thought up a new trick — this was later, in the third form, where you learn that phosphorus glows in the dark. He bought some from Herr Pexider (above his shop door hung a sign reading "Materialist," as druggists were sometimes called back then, and above it, curiously enough, a golden angel floating into abstraction, the symbol of this guild). He then daubed the phosphoric solution on the contours of the grandparents. His step, entering the room one evening at dusk, shrieked at the sight of these gleaming grimaces and in her shock dropped the kerosene lamp she'd just cleaned. Papa naturally gave the boy a good hiding, what else was he supposed to do. But the fluorescent faces of her ancestors remained this way for months. His parents continued to quarrel, scenes that made the walls shake. Step threatened suicide because of the phosphorescence, but finally let it be.

That was because the next day they were leaving on their summer vacation. (First class, express train, with the free family pass higher railroad officials were entitled to.) Final destination: Mies on the Miesa, an old Bohemian mining town whose silver shafts now only yielded lead glance. From there by mail coach through spruce forests to Kladrau, a farming village with an old monastery nearby. They stayed at Frau Martschin's, a hog trader's widow. There was also a daughter in the house, thirteen years old with a high-flying skirt and nothing underneath. She liked to be caught while playing tag, and the boy caught her thoroughly.

In the morning, backpack full of salami sandwiches, he accompanied his father to the forests to pick berries in logging areas, hunt mushrooms under young spruce, catch trout in the streams, and lounge in the sun in the clearings. None of that appealed to his step, who stayed home and made sour faces in the evening. Father and son hiked far, very far, all the way to Wolfsberg and Oschelin, passing through the places where his father had spent his childhood and youth. Nice here, isn't it? That's the call of a yellowhammer, and this is pyrite, looks like gold, that butterfly is a mourning cloak, look at the larkspurs here on the ground, and there's brown-black augite under the castle ruins at Wolfsberg. Goethe collected it there when he was older. (Not entirely true, what he said about the elderly Goethe, but it sounded impressive enough.) His father read from the story of Reynard the Fox and the boy hoped he would one day meet the famous baron in person. But only occasionally did he chance upon Lampe the Hare, or, if luck was on his side, see a deer pass by or a buck with palmed antlers.

They wandered through villages on hot afternoons. Not a soul in sight, everyone was in the fields. Even the tavern was empty, where a swaddled infant dangled on a rope suspended from a ceiling hook in the middle of the taproom. Passersby could give it a push and make it swing back and forth. "An ingenious invention to replace the cradle," explained the boy's father, demonstrating how it worked while the dangling child began to blare. But the father did his best to calm it: "Hush, little baby, you might be famous one day like Galileo or maybe just an ordinary scoundrel, what do I know? They rocked me back and forth like that too." But to his son he said: "You, of course, had to have a stupid stroller."

Once they even came to Hammermühle below Wolfsberg. His father fell silent, sat down at the edge of the forest and looked down at the millhouse from where the clatter of a wheel could be heard. "Aren't we going there, Father?" — but he didn't answer, and they went back into the woods.

The years lumbered by, one after the other, but his step remained his step. The boy grew into a young man and his methods of combat became less fierce, in deference to his aging father but also because of other distractions, and because he'd learned to wield the weapon of irony. The quarrels between his father and his step also became less frequent, but his family was still a far cry from being the "Home, Sweet Home" advertised in blue cross-stitch above the kitchen table. His father became more mellow and apathetic. His step, a decade younger, still stirred unremittingly in the simmering cauldron of discontent, but his father, when it became too much for him, just sat down at the piano and improvised a song from the *Regensburger Liederkranz*.

Over the years her nature had fully taken possession of her outward appearance, making her angular and jagged.

Pointed chin, pointed nose,
These are the devil's clothes,

his father offered by way of interpretation. When he entered retirement, the aging couple moved to the countryside to a little place called Weseritz, a mere two hours' walk from his father's place of birth nestled in the forest. So there he was, treading the ground of his childhood again, smelling the scent of his indigenous landscape, speaking with the locals in the language of his youth. Perhaps this homecoming was a belated admission of having made the grave mistake of leaving his native realm in the first place, having lived his entire life as a man, including his professional life and two ill-fated marriages, against the grain of his own nature, so that now, in the end, all that was left for him was at least to receive death at a place he could more or less rightly call his own. After all, one didn't give birth to oneself. The earth, air and light of the landscape were partly responsible too. He bore their heritage, but also their burden of debt. Here he had been a child, and this homeland had actively interfered in his childhood and youth. This homeland might have said: "Love me!" But its own obligations were no less when it came to love. And the boy's step? — They claim that people aren't born good or evil, that their innermost character is determined by a primal experience, the painstaking revelation and conscious realization of which can, under the right circumstances, change a person's nature. The evil that creeps or surges through the world is asttributed to a primordial terror. It's possible, then, that his step, too, had once been an innocent babe lying in a stroller or bassinet or swaddled and dangling from a rope from the ceiling of a taproom, until the evil eye fell on her and only left her with two modes of behavior: cowering defense or sneak attack. You can view it from a pathological perspective, but what do you gain by doing so? Nothing at least in the mind of a boy under siege, who has to defend himself against the unreasonable demands of a treacherous individual and who runs the risk of falling ill himself if he ever lays down his arms. Any assessment of her character needs to bear in mind that his step came from a small village inn with stables and fields. Nature, or so we are told, purifies and ennobles the soul. But not those who merely exploit it. His father, on the other hand, was the son of a schoolmaster and the grandson of a physician. For someone whose destiny was to be derailed by fatal errors in decision-making, it seems quite remarkable that his forebears had exclusively dedicated their lives to teaching what was right and just, to preventing mistakes and curing evils.

His father's end came unexpectedly. The son — the reader already knows it's me, so I'll openly acknowledge my identity — I had hoped and prayed that this house and garden in the countryside would grant my father at least a few more years of modest satisfaction. But he only lived to see one spring there, one summer and one fall. On Christmas morning — I had come for the holidays — the doctor said: "I'd urgently advise that you have the last rites performed . . . And perhaps," he added, "some brandy to boost his spirits." Father lay there staring into space. "Why so suddenly?" I asked myself with a shudder. He's not that old and was always so resilient. Step paced back and forth, acting conspicuously unconcerned. You have to die of something. Then my father looked at me at length, but I don't know if he saw me. Finally he said: "I have to die in a strange place." And those were his last words. Was this not his native soil all around him? All my step said was: "From now on I'll have milk with brandy every morning." Seldom have words been spoken with more profound sincerity.

Six railroad men carried him to the cemetery. A locomotive at the train station below whistled shrilly through the winter landscape while he was being lowered into his grave. The stationmaster's idea of a last salute. — "We bid a warm welcome to all those who've come to accompany our dear Chief Inspector on his last journey." One has to bear in mind that the speaker and most of the mourners had been drinking Schwamberger beer at the expense of the bereaved ever since the early morning. What a funeral! From the cemetery one could see across the plateaus to Radischerberg, the old hillfort, and beyond to the deer park, in which lay nestled the village where Father was born. "I have to die in a strange place!"

Putting the estate in order. My great-grandfather's parchment doctor's diploma, 1788. "We, the Director and Dean of the honorable Faculty of Medicine at the venerable Imperial and Royal Ferdinand University of Prague . . ." — Seigneurial appointment decree with large official seal: "By the grace of God, We, the reigning Prince of Löwenstein of the Holy Roman Empire, etc. . . ." from 1792. — My grandfather's schoolmaster's papers. Grandmother's love letters. "Worthiest friend!" My grandparents' prenuptial agreement: "First, both the bride and the bridegroom promise each other marital fidelity and love." Well, supposedly she wasn't all too faithful, Barbara, the goldbeater's daughter from Weseritz. I heard about someone who always came over when the schoolmaster was in the tavern. But still she was pious, as evidenced by her prayerbook with the metal crucifix on the leather cover and her entries on the endpapers.

"On October 28, 1845, we celebrated our big day in Weseritz. Father Johannes Gröschel married us in the Church of the Assumption of the Virgin Mary. May God give us happiness, bestow us with His blessings and grant us both long lives. Amen!" None of which stopped her from taking a lover later. "On February 11, 1847, Thursday at two in the afternoon, under the sign of Aquarius, Theresia Urzidil was born" . . . "On August 6, 1850, at one-thirty in the afternoon, Aloisa Urzidil was born under the sign of Leo" . . . "On January 7, 1854, Joseph Urzidil was born at three o'clock in the afternoon, Friday." That was my father.

Then all of his school report cards. In chronological order. Secondary school (non-classical) in Elbogen. (Goethe ate trout and fell in love with Ulrike there.) Technical university in Prague, the golden city of a hundred spires. He loved to talk about this, but also about how he went home during vacation, attending one parish fair after another, roaming through the mill valleys until he reached the Wolfsberg area. Later his profession, and ultimately his marriage, would keep him in the capital for good.

What a marriage! A man in his forties marries a widow with seven children. Had one with her himself, her eighth. That was me. It killed her. In the old photos she's a real beauty of course, delicate in her puff-sleeve dress, and not at all worn-out despite her many childbirths. Mother! All I actually know is her grave (Olšany, Cemetery VIII, section 6, no. 176 — what would the dead be without numbers!).

My father's patent documents for his technical inventions. A mechanical train-car coupling device, a locomotive smoke consumer, and an adding machine with a keypad, a metal arrow indicating the totals on a spiral-shaped scale. My father had imagination. He also painted some appealing little pictures and liked to mess around with music.

Cash receipts, IOU's, bundle after bundle of postal receipts for regular payments. To whom? A certain Elisabetha Forstner, beginning in 1875, five florins every month. That was a good deal of money back then. This went on for more than twenty years. I have to die in a strange place! Was this lurking in the dusk when you improvised on the piano? Did it drift over from the mill valleys below Wolfsberg? We could hear the clatter of a mill wheel. "Aren't we going there, Father?" But you turned back and we went into the woods.

Those parts were full of Forstners. By the time you died more than forty years had passed. Better to let bygones be bygones. Was it a boy? A girl? Brother, sister? Better to leave such things untouched. Still, my father's child. Maybe dead already. Father kept his secret locked up tight. No mean feat. I have to die in a strange place. The official secret of a lifetime (that is, until the postal receipts gave it away).

Division of property. House and yard to me — I was the one who had purchased this property for my father — with Step allowed to use part of it for the remainder of her life, the other rooms for a tenant who agrees to take care of the garden and in return is allowed to plant his cabbage and collect the fruit. An attic room reserved for me in the summer. Step puts on a sour face. She's suspicious of fair solutions, sits below the Sistine Madonna and grumbles. She's sure to pick a fight with the new tenant before long.

It wasn't long in coming. The renter packed up and left. Others came and went. Not a single summer for me in the house. In the end I found a buyer who was willing to shoulder the burden of sharing it with my step until her dying day. I sold the house together with Step. One year followed the other. All I ever heard about was her bickering with the new owner and that she'd moved away to her birthplace on the Elbe, in Czech country. I'd hoped that was that, but was sorely mistaken. The grand finale was yet to come, performed with a full orchestra. It began with a shrill ring of the doorbell one night and a telegram: "Come immediately. Severely ill." The wish of a dying woman, I thought at first. She's up to something, I thought a moment later. Forebodings of a witches' sabbath. I parried the attack like a real champion and simply stayed home.

Of course, I missed the grandiose climax. Someone relayed the message to me about how she had summoned every last ounce of strength to deliver the main blow. She knew she was dying and arranged for the great day of judgment. She cabled all her relatives to come and solemnly convened them in her sickroom. Two burning candles flanked the crucifix, the local notary seated at the foot of the bed, above him the virginal Holy Sistine Madonna. Step in voluminous sheets, hollow-cheeked in her life's diminuendo, could have had mercy on everyone, and indeed her sisters and nephews and nieces were shy and scared at first. My guess had been correct, though, for she'd been carefully planning the whole thing for years.

She lifted herself from her pillows and, with a piercing look, let the fun begin. "Tell me, Frieda, are you still the slut you used to be, ready to hop in the sack with anyone who knocks on the door? That'll get harder for you with time. Notary, write down five thousand for Frieda. And you, Albin, you've never had anything but debts anyway. Never did a decent thing in your life. I leave you three thousand for you to squander. No use cowering, Martha, you're the same. You'll likewise inherit three thousand. Holy Mary! For riffraff like you I've saved my whole life." — "You shouldn't get worked up," her sister hazards. — "Leave me be! — I'll get worked up when I want to. My stomach heaves just hearing you. Remember all the things you did to me. You took my best dress from the wardrobe, stole my hairpins . . ." — "But that was when we were girls, that was forty years ago, don't start with that . . ." — "Forty or not, you've always been that way. Notary, five thousand for her, no, just three thousand, three thousand is enough. But don't any of you think you'll get the money just like that. Notary, write down the condition. They all have to come to my funeral in deep mourning, all of them dressed in black, all with flowers to toss in the grave, everyone has to cry, those who don't cry get nothing, if so much as one of them doesn't cry everything goes to the Animal Welfare League. Where's Liddy?"

"But Liddy's been dead for eight years . . ." — "Right, she's dead. A runaway." — "But auntie, that's sinful." — "Dead then. Could have had three thousand if she'd waited." Exhausted, she sank back into the cushions, drawing circles in the air with one hand as if she were collecting something. Everyone hoped she would die now. But she didn't die just yet, and it seemed that the circular movements served the singular purpose of collecting one last imaginary bucketful of filth to dump on the head of the next heir in line.

That was me. She sat up a bit and suddenly yelled: "Hans!" No one spoke. "Where's Hans?" her voice rang out this time with all the energy she could muster. "He's sick in bed," someone finally said. "Liar," she said, "That's a lie" — and was certainly right about that. "You must calm down," ventured the notary. "Who asked you?" she roared. "Liar, he's just playing one last trick on me. Doesn't want to hear the unvarnished truth. Did everything to spite me, from beginning to end. Me, the most self-sacrificing person in the world, who only worked for others, who never had anything from life, oh, I'm far too good. Write down three thousand for him, and I hope he chokes on it. And I forbid him to come to my funeral, I forbid him to cry . . ." She sank back in dire disappointment. "What is the gentleman's title?" asked the notary, "I mean on account of the address." And, with all the strength left inside her, she lifted herself up like a ghost and shrieked: "He doesn't have a title! They threw him out!" Those were her last words, and maybe her only real joy. And this was the message I received about her death.

Years came and went. Violence reigned. War broke out. Homelands were destroyed. Peoples uprooted. I've lived and still live in distant lands. In the heart of a distant place, that's where I'm at home. My step became a myth, and it is not out of rancor that this chronicle of her is being written but the simple recognition that people can be that way, that many people probably are. But one thing at least speaks in her favor: the evil that most people hide, yet go on committing all the same, was at least in plain view in the case of my step.

Life has the strange ability to round itself out, to harmonize and fill ancient gaps. One day, just as another war was over, or seemed to be, a letter reached me from the Old World. "Permit me, a stranger, to ask you the following question. I found your name in a magazine. Investigations necessitated during the war revealed to me that this name was that of my father as well. My mother, Elisabeth Forstner, whose name I bear, never spoke to me about him. And yet I'd be glad to know if you and my father are related. I'm seventy-two years old and was born in a mill at the foot of Wolfsberg . . ."

De profundis! You, oh Lord, ordain things according to Your counsel and keep them safe in the depths of Your power. You allow them to ripen according to Your Law and manifest them as You see fit. Evil does not offend You, for its wages aren't here but there; and the good man does not impress You, for You Yourself created him to be good. But with the smile of unity You have blessed all the world, and promised through the holiness of redemption to heal all wounds.

Oh my father, why did you abandon your beloved, with her child and yours? The girl from the mill, she was surely made for you. She was no fling, no misguided fit of passion. You sat with me at the edge of the forest and gazed into the valley with the mill. I saw the look in your eyes. You might have fooled a good many people, maybe even yourself, but not me, your child. When a child sees his father crying, he suddenly sees the child in his father, and feels a deep kinship with him.

You, the young student, had won her over. You walked together through green fields and forests, lay in the shadows, and God was with you both. Then you came no more, and she pleaded with the forests and the heavens, the wrath of her parents descended on her, and she gave birth like a creature of the woods. You dreamed a different life, the guilt was on you and you knew it: I have to die in a strange place.

You took the wrong path, and I'm the child of this error. I know I wouldn't exist if you'd been faithful to her. But was it really so important for me to exist? Just so that one day I could close the circle and wind back the error to where it began? Was it so important for me to exist, I don't want to blaspheme, but it need not have been, not for all the joys of my life and not for all the suffering. You would have lived with the daughter of the valley and delighted in your son. But I hear you say: Whose life is in his own hands?

And yet the life you lived I can only accept with humility. I took the place of the one you rejected, shared your gloom and suffered your benevolent fury. Perhaps I sensed that your strictness was not really meant for me and that your benevolence missed the mark when it was aimed at me. I couldn't see your guilt, but your atonement didn't escape me.

I have before me a picture of your son, who resembles you more than I ever did. He has your eyes, your mouth, your forehead, and probably your voice and movements, too. He even had the occupation you wished for when you were young. You wanted to be a farmer. Why didn't you become one? Why did you study strange things and become a stranger to yourself? Why did you marry strangers and father a strange child? While your own lay hidden in a drawer in the form of money orders. I now understand my vague suspicion when you hit me and it somehow didn't really hurt.

We exchange letters, my half-brother and I. I describe to him his father, the way he looked, the way he lived, his fate, his habits, and how he loved the landscape of his youth. I tell him about myself, about the early death of my mother and that, just as he had no father, I was destined to have no mother. He lost his native forests and lived in a strange place. My homeland is what I write. He's old. Almost old enough to be my father. But neither am I so young anymore.

One day we discover that the people whose familiar presence shaped our lives for better or for worse and who helped make us who we are, one day we discover that these people are no longer there, and that we talk about a quarter of a century as casually as if it were two years or five. The things that once concerned us deeply have now become trivial, and many things we treated with aloofness and fancied ourselves immune to are now demanding their due, and all we can do is bow our heads in silence.

One day we realize that something unspeakably grave is fast approaching and wants to enter our consciousness. One day we understand the meaning of goodbyes. One day! Actually just a split second of that day, a wholly indifferent, prosaic and unpathetic second, maybe while lifting a glass to our mouth or sharpening a pencil or shifting in a chair, or maybe doing nothing at all but sitting and staring into space.

Father, you didn't like that I became a writer. But maybe it had to be that way so that your son would find me, across generations and oceans, and so I could tell him about you.

PATERNAL PRAGUE

The obvious contradictions in the nature and behavior of my father presumably had a stimulating effect on my development. They say a consistent character sets an example for others. Inconsistency, though, presents a more truthful picture of life. My father was a rare and ordinary person. When I was a boy of six, he lulled me to sleep every evening by reading to me from Wieland's *Oberon* and *History of the Abderites*. And yet until my sixteenth birthday he forbade me from reading at all before bedtime lest it should keep me awake at night. He could even become so violent that he'd tear up harmless books borrowed from my classmates and chuck them into the stove. I then had to replace them with money from my meager allowance.

My father considered himself a good Catholic but never went to Mass on Sunday, let alone Easter Confession and Communion. Even so, he insisted that I practice Catholicism, and was extraordinarily pleased when I served as an altar boy at church. This notwithstanding, he took me to synagogues, Protestant and Russian Orthodox churches, and claimed that all religions were equal. If Prague had had a mosque or a Shinto temple, he would have taken me there, too, to prove to me the equality of all confessions and creeds.

My father Josef Urzidil, born in 1854 in Schippin, a secluded forest settlement in the western part of Bohemia, the son of the local school-teacher, was not very fond of Jews and on occasion even went so far as to describe himself as an "anti-Semite," which in no way prevented him from marrying a beautiful Jewish woman from Prague, who brought with her from her previous, Jewish marriage no less than seven children and with whom he begat a son, Johannes Urzidil. She died a mere four years later. When, at the age of twenty-six, this son took as his wife the daughter of an Orthodox rabbi, his "anti-Semitic" father said: "I like the young lady, a lot. But you'll have a hard time with her family."

My father was a German nationalist, and proudly exchanged the greeting "Hail Pan-Germany!" with parliamentarian Schönerer, the most radical chauvinist in all of Bohemia. My father was what they called a "Czech-eater," and although he lived for forty years among the Czechs of Prague, he neither spoke nor understood a single word of their language. And yet he gave me strict orders to learn the Czech language myself, indeed his second marriage was to an enthusiastic Czech nationalist, with whom he found himself in perpetual plate-slinging conflict, arguing day and night not just about family matters but also about politics, dragging me in as well of course — me, who waged a vehement war against my stepmother using every dirty trick in the book, or sometimes, depending on the day, tore her away from the window of our fourth-floor apartment (not counting the mezzanine) just as she threatened to plunge to her death.

My father was deeply moral. He inveighed against Émile Zola (placing the accent on the first syllable: Zóla), spurning in particular his novel *The Sin of Abbé Mouret.* And yet, after my father's death, it suddenly came to light that he'd sired an illegitimate son with a Sudeten German girl. I'm presently in cordial correspondence with this child — a situation my father had surely never imagined.

My father was a passionate railroad official. He used the red material of his uniform cap as a decorative covering on the cross of a crucifix hanging over his bed. And although he was entitled to the benefit of free travel (later even in first class) on all state railways of the Austro-Hungarian Empire, including the Adriatic Lloyd and the Danube Steamship Company, he never, with one single exception, availed himself of this opportunity, unfailingly choosing instead to spend our summer vacations in the vicinity of his native village in western Bohemia, a little over ninety miles from Prague, two hours away by express train. The one exception was his "honeymoon" with my Czech stepmother, to Vienna and Salzburg, on which occasion I was taken along — I was eight years old at the time — and which I recollect with dread, for the newlyweds fought at Schönbrunn Zoo no less than at Hohensalzburg Fortress. My rustic father hollered at my stepmother outside Mozart's birthplace, informing her that she was "an unmusical idiot born in a cowshed." The scorned woman shouted back that my father was born in a zoo, which technically was true, for the little village of Schippin, consisting of a little church, presbytery, school, forester's lodge, and tavern, was actually located in the middle of the (incidentally wonderful) Prince Löwenstein game reserve near Weseritz in western Bohemia, and — despite its seclusion — formed a small parish incorporating several of the surrounding villages.

My father had a republican streak, but was loyal to the Emperor all the same. He felt like an Austrian (in a monarchical way) but still admired Bismarck. He used to proudly show off the thaler coin the Iron Chancellor had given him back when he was a twelve-year-old boy. What for? This is the storybook tale he told: "On the very day of the Battle of Königgrätz, my father and I went for a walk nearby. Taking our lunch in the open country, a group of horsemen stopped before us. One of them, a towering man, bent down from his horse to ask if we might spare a slice of bread and sausage. My father offered him one, and he in turn handed it to a full-bearded gentleman with the words, 'Here, Your Majesty.' Then he turned to me: 'Here's a thaler from the King of Prussia.' Those kings, they've got it in them." And yet, in 1918, when the Habsburg monarchy collapsed and the Czechoslovak Republic was proclaimed, I heard my father say: "Good riddance to all those counts and princes. We won't be saying 'Your Highness' and nonsense like that anymore. In a republic you don't say 'madam,' either, except to a baroness or countess of course."

As the son of a village schoolmaster, who doubled as a church organist and music teacher, my father had learned since childhood to play a variety of musical instruments. He was an accomplished piano, flute and violin player, and he spoke admiringly of the great masters. "Mozart, Beethoven and Schubert: now that's music. Everything else is humbug." Sitting down at the piano, though, he'd play "A Maiden's Prayer," "Egerlanders, Stick Together," and "The Dream of a Reservist."

My father loved me. I always felt and knew it. But if we were gathering mushrooms and he caught me pulling up porcini by the roots, instead of gently slicing them off at the stem, he'd become so enraged that he'd fling his long sharp Bosniak knife at me and I'd hear it whizzing past, a hair's breadth away from me — quite intentionally, by the way, for he aimed to miss with precision. If he wanted to he could aim to hit, and would spear river trout with the very same knife instead of fishing for them like others did. He was not the kind of person to lie in wait with murderous intent, but attacked the trout like a lion its prey. Humans had a right to mushrooms and trout, but pulling a mushroom up by the root was no less criminal than throwing away a crust of bread. Woe to you! A gift from God! It was hard in those moments to come away unscathed. He was a friend of nature who knew every plant, stone, insect and woodland creature down to the very last detail, and who taught me how to mimic the call of any wild bird.

Despite his being at war with my step — indeed he seemed to have married her for this very purpose, the two of them always going at it in my presence, hurling the most obscene expressions at each other — he strictly forbade me to behave toward her in a way that was even remotely offensive, however much this woman tormented me. That was his prerogative. If I did so despite his warnings, I was not only slapped in the face but often got a sound thrashing, administered to me with the triple-edged, inlaid rococo dagger conveniently hanging on the wall and that used to belong to my great-grandfather, the father of my grandmother, who in his day had once been a physician in the employ of Prince Löwenstein, an occupation that back in those days evidently called for wearing a dagger to boost one's credibility.

His reading of Wieland to me aside, my father did not care much for poetry or literature. He referred to them as "useless chatter and a waste of time." But when at the age of seventeen I had my first poems published in this or that newspaper he carefully clipped them out and kept them in his breast pocket so he could proudly show them off to his pals at the tavern. "You put that one together quite nicely," he said, without having understood a single line of my highly expressionist utterances.

I could easily list a hundred examples of contradictions, discrepancies and contrasts in my father's nature. And yet if someone claimed he was a muddleheaded person who must have been inscrutable, absurd and hateful to a growing boy like me, I would have to object vehemently. I viewed my father as a brightly colored, ever-changing kaleidoscope. Never did I write him an accusatory letter, because he didn't make me suffer, however much his incalculable despotism and sheer brute force provided a counterpoint in my life. I rather loved being punished by him for my never-ending misdemeanors. We were sovereign partners in this regard, and the walloping was an integral part of this, the corroboration of my misdeeds. The harder the smack, the more deeply I was convinced that I'd said or done the right thing to my stepmother.

I appreciated my father's wild and violent vitality, which I've probably inherited enough of to get myself into trouble but never to suddenly find myself in a drowsy philistine rut. It may be correct that the mark of civilization is restraint and self-control, but these are likewise sources of hypocrisy and insincerity, behaviors utterly alien to my father. He lived two lives and both of them with pleasure, a genial one and a brutal one, very much at home and mindful in each; he never mixed them up, and certainly didn't suffer from any such ambivalence. He could content himself with a cup of hibiscus tea, but could just as well guzzle twelve beers in one sitting; and after the soothing hibiscus tea he could rage like an angry boar at the Czechs or Jews, whereas after the twelfth glass of beer he could preach national reconciliation with Franciscan tenderness and praise the chief rabbi of Prague as a paragon of *kalokagathia*. Of course, the whole thing could just as well play out the other way around, and this complete unpredictability had a colossal romantic and adventurous appeal to me. Father comes home from the office. What will it be today? What surprises are awaiting us? Nobody knew.

Josef Urzidil had graduated from a *Realschule* — a modern secondary school without instruction in the classics — and later went to Prague Technical University, where he earned a degree in engineering. Apart from his job at the railways, he was also an inspired technical inventor. He is credited with developing an adding machine with a keypad, a mechanical train-car coupling device, and a locomotive smoke consumer, each one now long since obsolete but which in their day were patented inventions in Austria and Germany. He enrolled me, his son, in a humanistic Gymnasium, because "a person needs to know some Latin and Greek, otherwise he doesn't have an education." Yet not a moment later he'd say: "Technology, physics, mathematics and mechanical engineering rule the world nowadays." He probably didn't expect me to rule the world or want to. He taught me how to read when I was five years old, first with the help of the satiric *Fliegende Blätter* magazine, where I learned to spell out jokes ("Oh, these stepmothers!" or "Oh, these bachelors!"), then with the aid of a journal called *Bahn frei* (Clear the Tracks!), published by the Association of Austrian Railway Officials for its members. My first experience with literature was an essay in the latter on "Urzidil's Locomotive Smoke Consumer," in which the name of the inventor was mentioned multiple times. "You see," he said, "that's what I call going places." Later I was allowed to move on to more classic texts, for example the *Service Regulations for Transportation on the Imperial and Royal Austrian State Railways.* I learned the technical jargon so well that thirty years later, as a German interpreter at state negotiations concerning a German–Czech Railway Agreement, I was able to astonish the Czech railway minister with my detailed knowledge of the terminology. "Where did you learn all that?" he asked in amazement. "I learned how to read from the *Regulations for Transportation.*" Perhaps it is true of my father that he was stranger and more bizarre than fathers ordinarily tend to be in the eyes of their children. But this added element of the strange and bizarre was not merely the result of, say, my generation having outgrown his, as is normally the case. True, I may have mocked him, but I also felt a wholesome fear of him. Both of these are attitudes you should always adopt toward life. My father presumably feared me too in his own way, and probably found me just as unusual, strange and bizarre as I did him. He feared me because he was a widower from the time I was four years old and, even for many years after he'd remarried, felt the need to replace my mother. Being a father is hard enough, but trying to combine it with being a surrogate mother is bound to go wrong at some point. He compensated this disparity by affecting a certain disdainfulness toward the opposite sex.

"You're thirteen now. Come, let's go for a walk. We'll have a little chat about women. Now then, women. Every month they have this unpleasant business ... Perhaps it's best not to talk about it." Luckily I was streetwise enough when it came to the female mysteries and more or less knew the ropes (or didn't).

"What's that, a sore throat? There's only one cure for that: Alum gargle!" (As soon as he started talking like that I knew it was getting dangerous.)

"No, not the alum!," I bleated.

"Then you'll go straight to the doctor for me!" (Doing things "for him" was even more dangerous.)

"No, not to the doctor!" I yowled.

"Off you go to Doctor Pauli! Pauli was an Imperial and Royal regimental physician during the occupation of Bosnia. Schiller's father was also a regimental physician."

"Who's Schiller?"

"That's not important right now. His father, anyway, was a regimental physician. Your great-grandfather was a doctor too. If he hadn't been a doctor, you wouldn't have even been born."

"Why would I have not been born?"

"Because he'd planned on becoming a Catholic priest before he switched to medicine."

"And why would I have not been born if my great-grandfather had become a Catholic priest?"

"Don't ask stupid questions." The sin of Abbé Mouret was probably still simmering in my father's mind. That's how our conversations went. But every son has more questions than his father can answer or thinks he can answer. This is the source of progress from one generation to the next. Poets tend to fall far from the tree. Rilke's father was a railroad official like mine. My father pointed him out to me once on Prague's Herrengasse, when I was still in grammar school. "That's

Chief Inspector Rilke," he said, bowing deeply, "they say his son is some kind of poet." Werfel's father was a glove manufacturer. He would always greet you with a line from Gustav Freytag's *Debit and Credit,* delivered in the very same tone each time: "Bad times, bad times! Business is languishing." And Kafka's father? Good God! A tyrannical, card-playing petty bourgeois, but that was nothing special. Like most fathers of his ilk, he was no subject worthy of a literary indictment, which he never received anyway. The principle question is always whether the characteristics of your father amuse you or depress you. In my case it was both, and the mixture produced a kind of joyful melancholy. To be sure, the generation of fathers in the era of Emperor Franz Joseph did not have to make the weighty decisions of conscience that later fathers did. Hence my father could afford to be *for* something one time and *against* the very same thing another. It wasn't a matter of life or death back then, and — take him for all in all — his being for something one time and against it another proved to be a kind of "emotional objectivity" and was, strictly speaking, better than never being for or against anything. (The latter was actually the reason why Kafka inwardly resented his father.) And this "emotional objectivity" was certainly better than pigheaded totalitarian behavior of any hue.

My father, who outlived Emperor Franz Joseph by six years, never had a political discussion with me, even though when he passed away I was already twenty-six years old and worked in a diplomatic, that is to say, a political office. At the age of nineteen I was a contributor to Franz Pfemfert's *Aktion*, meaning my sympathies were clearly with the left. But that meant nothing to my father. There were poor people and there were rich people. "You always have the poor with you. Poverty is splendor from within," said Rilke, son of the railway man. And wealth alone doesn't make a person happy either. People talked about the "working poor," because workers, however much they toiled, were always poor, and indeed it had to be that way, because poverty, to fulfill its mission, needed not only an ideological but also a practical foundation. An Austrian state official — except if he were a minister — was not exactly "poor," but he was — as a matter of custom, so to speak — "impecunious." This moral was reflected in day-to-day speech. A Czech schoolbook put it this way: "The minister has a consort; the clerk has a spouse; the worker has a missus." A factory owner was naturally rich. I say "naturally" because back in the third form my classmate Fritz Gerstel, in response to my question "What do you want to be when you're older?" answered: "A factory owner, naturally, just like my old man." Nature was in league with the factory owner in an elemental way, as it were. At the age of nineteen I was deeply distressed by social issues, whereas my father at the age of sixty was utterly indifferent to them. National disputes, on the other hand, could make him livid with rage. The question of whether a train-station sign should be in German or in Czech or bilingual, or whether the Queen's Court Manuscript was early medieval or a Czech forgery could rob him of his sleep at night. Those were the days. Noses were bloodied on account of such things, but no one died because of them. Blows were exchanged on the streets of Prague when they introduced universal suffrage, too. Though, granted, this issue also had a distinctly national flavor. Yet no matter how vehement these clashes were, they never reached the point of murderousness. When all was said and done, state officials always had their Emperor and the conviction that "Austria will stand forever," or so the national anthem went, put to music by no less than Joseph Haydn, and sung by Czechs as well, albeit ironically.

What deeply preoccupied my father was the price of Pilsner, whether a pint cost twelve or thirteen kreutzers. Kafka's father was concerned about the price per meter of cotton or calico, and Werfel's father about the trade and traffic in buckskin gloves — genuine trade and traffic, for they were manufactured in Moravia then shipped to England and furnished with an English stamp before being reimported back to Bohemia. That's what I heard, anyway. To hell with universal suffrage! My father was a real "economizer," he treated himself and his family to just about nothing, investing what he had scrimped and saved in war bonds of all things, which in the end were rendered worthless, and rightly so. I never had new pants as a child, but only the kind that were patched together from my father's old, threadbare trousers. That was my contribution to Austrian war bonds. My father was stingy and suspicious, like a peasant character in Anzengruber, and all I could do was smile when after his death I discovered that for years he'd been paying child support for an illegitimate son. He'd probably worked out that child support was cheaper than getting married, a conclusion that has something to be said for it, and later was confirmed for him when the cloth business my mother had brought into the marriage soon went woefully bankrupt. It was bound to be that way, and one shouldn't refute oneself. If he'd married the village girl from Egerland, the one he had fathered a son with, then, true enough, I wouldn't exist — at least not in my present form — but he, for his part, would have saved himself untold trouble and heartache, not to mention a lot of unnecessary expenses. Admittedly, it's unlikely anyone else would have written an essay about him. That's why I don't hold it against him, and if I do reproach him posthumously for this or that or whatever, then it's not for my sake but his. I loved and still love his incoherencies and inconsistencies, his kind of Jekyll and Hyde existence. His birthplace, Schippin, which he himself painted with loving precision in oils in 1902, hangs in my room in such a way that I see it every day whenever I go to bed at night and wake up in the morning. Bereft of this daily encounter, I would take no pleasure in sleeping or waking. The village itself no longer exists. The expulsion of the Sudeten Germans caused it to fall into ruin, and the Czechs who took their place had no desire to start a new life within those ruined walls. Only in this little oil painting does Schippin still exist, as well as in some of my stories. The same goes for my father, this kaleidoscopic, quirky, grotesque, inventive fiend, whom I largely — so it would seem — take after.

When he went into retirement, I used my first savings from work to buy him a little house in the immediate vicinity of his native village, which he could easily reach on quiet paths through an Eichendorffian wooded valley. God knows one couldn't live in a place that was any more homey than that. But barely six months later he died there in my arms, on Christmas Eve, bizarrely muttering the following words to me: "So I have to die in a strange place." This, to me, was a hurtful inconsistency, and so, since sons have the privilege of contradicting posthumously, I had the following chiseled into his gravestone: "Rest in peace in your native soil." But paying a visit to his grave once later I was put in mind of the then fresh verses of my friend and fellow Praguer Franz Werfel, in refutation of my defiant epitaph:

Mothers exist so they one day vanish,
And the house we live in so it may fall,
Blest glances so their passing we lament.
Our heart's very beating is to us lent.
We are strangers here on this planet all,
And the things we tie ourselves to perish.

"People end up in foreign countries. Homesickness is their nourish-
ment, memories are their strength." These prescient lines were penned
by Johannes Urzidil in 1936, a few years before he himself wound up
in a foreign country. In the summer of 1939, the Bohemian-born
writer escaped from German-occupied Prague with the aid of a forged
passport, heading, via Trieste and Genoa, to London and from there
to the English countryside. He was forty-three years old at the time
and looked back on a productive career as a journalist, critic, translator
and poet in "Golden Prague" between the two world wars. In February
1941, he arrived by ship on the icy shores of New York, surviving
German torpedo attacks along the way and eventually settling in
Queens. In the New World he flourished as a fiction writer — wholly
invisible as a public figure in his host culture, as he never abandoned
his native German. "I've lived and still live in distant lands. In the heart
of a distant place, that's where I'm at home."

Born on February 3, 1896, on Krakauergasse (Krakovská Street) just
off Wenceslas Square in Prague, the capital of the Kingdom of
Bohemia in multiethnic Austria-Hungary, Urzidil was a child of his
era and environment — a place of literary lore and ambition, at least
for the dominant minority, the German-speaking middle class. The

gynecologist assisting at his birth was none other than Hugo Salus, an accomplished Prague poet and story writer, "the acknowledged pope of the [literary] establishment" in turn-of-the-century Prague, as Ernst Pawel has it. Urzidil published his first poems in the *Prager Tagblatt* at the age of seventeen, and began frequenting Café Arco soon after, becoming associated with the so-called Prague Circle that included poet and novelist Franz Werfel, polymath Max Brod (a "veritable literary cosmos," writes Urzidil), authors Ernst Weiss, Ludwig Winder and Oskar Baum, philosophers Felix Weltsch and Hugo Bergmann, and of course Franz Kafka. Urzidil later had the honor of holding one of three funeral orations for Kafka in 1924, predicting his future fame.

His first book, *Fall of the Damned,* a volume of poetry, was published in 1919 by Kurt Wolff in Leipzig as No. 65 in the legendary "Day of Judgment" series alongside Kafka's *Metamorphosis*, which appeared a few years earlier. This brief Expressionist phase included short stories, at least half a dozen of which were published in newspapers and anthologies between 1918 and 1920. In 1919, he cofounded with Winder the German Writers Union of Czechoslovakia and served as its managing director till 1933, when he resigned in protest over political tensions within the group. From 1919 to 1933 he worked at the German Embassy in Prague, first as a translator, later as its press attaché. He even took German citizenship in 1930, until the new Germans, those of the thousand-year Reich, had no use for him anymore, his mother having been Jewish. (She died when he was four, and his father, a Sudeten-German railroad official and inventor, later married a bristly Czech nationalist from Nymburk.)

Out of work, mistrusted by Germans and Czechs alike, Urzidil spent much of the thirties writing for the drawer in a village in the Western Bohemian countryside close to the birthplace of his father. His 1932 monograph *Goethe in Bohemia* would eventually save his life by bringing him to the attention of his future benefactress, the shipping heiress Winifred Ellerman, alias Bryher — English novelist, patient of Freud, rescuer of over a hundred imperiled intellectuals in Nazi-occupied Europe, Urzidil among them. Urzidil endeavored to repay the favor, dedicating three of his books to her and even translating a volume of verse by her partner H.D. (Hilde Doolittle).

Life in America was harsh at first. His meager income as a journalist, writing for Czech émigré periodicals in London, was not enough to make ends meet. And so he resorted to working as a self-employed, self-taught leather craftsman, manufacturing little decorative boxes, sometimes hundreds in a matter of weeks, even jeopardizing his health in the process. His wife, Gertrude, herself a poet, earned money as a babysitter. They had no children.

> I don't want to describe the many tribulations of exile, individual hopes that were dashed, the many failed attempts, and the phases of emotional and spiritual depression. These are trivialities of emigration and belong to the category of "ignoble misfortune," as my old friend Max Brod once put it quite aptly. And yet the case of a writer seems particularly difficult when he is determined to stick to his mother or father tongue as the sole legitimate and consummate expression of his world of ideas, and doggedly refuses to write in an acquired language. Nevertheless, we somehow managed to get by from month to month. We've never been all that vulnerable, Gertrude and I, since we don't mind living in poverty.

Poverty, relatively speaking, was nothing new to Urzidil. While his German-speaking, mostly Jewish friends and colleagues in late Habsburg Austria generally belonged to the bourgeois "Stadtpark society," he grew up in the working-class neighborhoods of Žižkov and Karlín. He would later quip, "I'm on the side of the poor, for theirs is the kingdom of heaven and also the kingdom of poets."

His decision to continue working in German, the "language of the murderers," whose race laws had classified him as a half-Jew, was hardly an auspicious one. But his reasons for holding on to his language were not just pragmatic — his advanced age and minimal knowledge of English — they were also deeply personal: "German is my beloved language . . . It is the very element of my being, my living mother to whom I have professed my undying loyalty in my most difficult hours of exile, in the darkest and most dubious hours of Germanness itself, when nothing I wrote had a chance of being published." Indeed, he even viewed it as a kind of ethical imperative: "The love of my language as my spiritual source of life gives me an obligation to those who belong to it," the community of German speakers, many of whom "stand in the shadow of a sin committed against the spirit of this language."

In one of his American stories, the masterful "Death and Taxes" from 1964, Urzidil tells the tale of Franz Lampenstein, an aging immigrant file clerk in New York who prefers to consider himself a poet, even adopting the pen name Frank Stonelight when he begins to write and publish in English. In an act of artistic hubris, he declares this poetry his main occupation, thus running afoul of the IRS when he tries to claim his bedroom as an office: "Stonelight became unsure of himself, for he knew well enough that poetry isn't written in a room per se but in the world at large, and that the finest ideas and lines come to you not so much in a room but when you're out walking, so that he basically would have had to deduct the whole world in his tax return." This *luftmensch* is arguably a foil for the path Urzidil didn't take. Whereas Lampenstein made the switch to English, transforming himself into "Stonelight" and becoming a buffoon in the process, Urzidil remained firmly rooted in German and wrote for the Old World, or what was left of it, despite his ambivalence toward his readers ("I can't shake the notion that the concentration camp is merely the flipside of the summer cottage, and that Hitler was most agreeable to the true German soul").

After a brief stint as a radio scriptwriter and information specialist for the Austrian division of Voice of America from 1951 to 1953 — his first steady income and full-time job since being forced to leave the German Embassy in Prague — he finally returned to Europe on a visit with the aim of finding a publisher. Success was soon to follow. His literary breakthrough came in 1956, at the age of sixty, with the publication in Munich of a collection of autobiographical stories entitled *The Lost Beloved*. This was followed in 1959 by his only full-fledged novel, *The Great Hallelujah*, set in America of the 1940s, a roman à clef of the German-speaking community of exiles gathered in Vermont and New York around journalist Dorothy Thompson, who counted among his closest friends in America.

The 1960s, his most prolific decade, began with the publication of a much-hailed volume of stories, *The Prague Triptych*. Numerous book publications followed, more or less haphazard collections appearing in rapid succession and often blurring the line between fiction, autobiography and essay. Of his seventy-some stories, more novella-like than short, about two-thirds take place in prewar Prague and Bohemia. His American stories, mostly set in New York City, make up roughly a quarter of his fictional output. Other occasional settings include antiquity, Britain, Italy, and Basque Country during the Spanish Civil War. But it was Urzidil's Bohemian stories that ultimately established his reputation.

A writer with a strong sense of language and place, Urzidil's work was positively *urig* — earthy, rustic, rooted — which probably hasn't served him well as an international literary passport. Claudio Magris, one of Urzidil's early admirers outside the German-speaking world, who arranged the first translations into Italian during the writer's lifetime, characterized Urzidil's relation to Bohemia as such: "Johannes

Urzidil . . . had decided to take this multinational homeland with him, to turn himself into his homeland and continue to copiously draw from it the ferment of his life and his art." Stone by stone, he diligently rebuilt his native Prague, reclaiming the places and people that history took away from him and he would never see again. Or to use a very Bohemian and Stifteresque metaphor: he transformed the spiritual impoverishment of a life in exile into little sparkling gems, revealing through his art an unexpected "splendor from within."

"Was he old-fashioned?" asked the great Kafka scholar and editor Heinz Politzer. "He was a natural storyteller and never posed the question." Viennese critic and grande dame Hilde Spiel remarked that his work had "an exceptional human warmth, a truly charismatic radiance." In an obituary two days after his death in November 1970, three months shy of his seventy-fifth birthday, she wrote:

> Undoubtedly Urzidil was one of the last great storytellers of the classic mold, a spinner of yarns of the highest order whose clear, pure and transparent style had a vividness that was inherently and eminently meaningful. If one wanted to characterize his prose, the best epithets would be beautiful, wise, unhurried. But it also had a fourth dimension, the mystical-mythical-fantastic component unique to all Prague German writers, the gift of their grand and venerable, their golden and uncanny city.

Peter Demetz described him as a man of stupendous learning, adding: "The most erudite of all Prague German writers, his mastery consists not least of all in his ability to tell a story while politely concealing his erudition." He refers to Urzidil elsewhere as a "Bohemian Homerid," whose modernity lay in "the fragile boundary between the epic and the essay."

The stories gathered here in English — fragments of a vast and scattered memoir, which this volume attempts to put together into a more coherent whole — are taken from five different German publications, culling the best from his first collection and adding key pieces written later in life, filling out the mosaic, so to speak, of his autobiographical project. Though not chronological in their order of original publication, they are chronological in setting.

The penultimate story, "Step and Half," an outlier here with its collage-like elements and abrupt narrative shift, is nonetheless representative of Urzidil's Bohemian stories in general. More than a reckoning with his almost cartoonishly wicked stepmother, it's a poignant study of loss and failure, questioning the very root of existence in the face of a life gone sour, his father's, but also reaffirming the redemptive power of art in the face of the messy business of life.

"Literature, today more than ever, has the task of keeping the world intellectually aware," he wrote in 1965 in a book-length essay, *Literature as Creative Responsibility*. "If it has a mission, this can only be to prevent the suicide of humanity." This claim seems more timely than ever. Calm, observant and humane, Urzidil's is a voice that can lead us through our darkest hours and remind us what it means to be human.

David Burnett
Leipzig, June 2022

JOHANNES URZIDIL (1896-1970) was a German-Czech-Jewish writer, poet, historian, and journalist. Born in Prague, he was the youngest member of the Prague Circle and a friend of Franz Kafka, later penning a collection of essays about him, *There Goes Kafka*. When Nazi Germany occupied Bohemia and Moravia in 1939, he and his wife, the daughter of an Orthodox rabbi, first fled to England before later moving to the United States. He started publishing fiction later in life, and is best known for the collection *The Lost Beloved* and the novel in stories *The Prague Triptych*. Urzidil won a number of awards for his writing and has an asteroid named after him.

DAVID BURNETT, a native of Cleveland, Ohio, has lived since the mid-1990s in Leipzig, Germany, where he works as a translator. He was a 2018 Translation Fellow of the National Endowment of the Arts (NEA) and received a 2014 PEN/Heim Translation Fund grant for his work on Johannes Urzidil's stories. Having translated the collections *The Last Bell* and *House of the Nine Devils*, Burnett is currently completing the first ever English translation of Urzidil's masterpiece *The Prague Triptych*.

HOUSE OF THE NINE DEVILS
Selected Bohemian Tales
by Johannes Urzidil

Translated by David Burnett from the original German

Frontispiece and cover image (Prague, 1890s) by Jindřich Eckert
courtesy of the Jewish Museum in Prague
Cover and design by Silk Mountain
Set in Garamond Pro

FIRST EDITION

Published by Twisted Spoon Press in 2022

P.O. Box 21 — Preslova 12
150 00 Prague 5
Czech Republic
www.twistedspoon.com

Printed and bound in the Czech Republic by Akcent

UK & Europe trade distribution:
CENTRAL BOOKS
www.centralbooks.com

US & Canada trade distribution:
SCB DISTRIBUTORS
www.scbdistributors.com

"House of the Nine Devils" was first published as "Zu den neun Teufeln," in *Das Elefantenblatt* (Munich: Langen-Müller, 1962); "Vacation in Flames" as "Flammende Ferien," "New Year's Commotion" as "Neujahrsrummel," "Porter Kubat" as "Dienstmann Kubat," "A Night of Terror" as "Eine Schreckensnacht," "One Last Deed" as "Ein letzter Dienst," and "Step and Half" as "Stief und Halb," in *Die verlorene Geliebte* (Munich: Langen-Müller, 1956); "We Stood Honor Guard" as "Wir standen Spalier" and "The Assassin" as "Der Attentäter," in *Bekenntnisse eines Pedanten* (Zurich: Artemis, 1972); "The Last Tombola" as "Die letzte Tombola," in *Die letzte Tombola* (Zurich: Artemis, 1971); "Paternal Prague" as "Väterliches aus Prag," in *Väterliches aus Prag, Handwerkliches aus New York* (Zurich: Artemis, 1969).